R.D. VILLAM

Brunhilde: Redemption

Copyright © 2023 by R.D. Villam

All rights reserved. No part of this publication may be reproduced, stored or transmitted in any form or by any means, electronic, mechanical, photocopying, recording, scanning, or otherwise without written permission from the publisher. It is illegal to copy this book, post it to a website, or distribute it by any other means without permission.

First edition

*This book was professionally typeset on Reedsy.
Find out more at reedsy.com*

Contents

Foreword — iv

1. The Isle of Forgotten Heroes — 1
2. The Serpent of the North Sea — 6
3. The Warmth of the Mead Hall — 11
4. The Weight of Our Choices — 16
5. The Journey to the Mountain — 21
6. The Heart of the Stronghold — 26
7. The Courage of the Dwarves — 31
8. The Ghost from the Past — 36
9. The Hope to Rise Again — 41
10. The Dwelling of the Goddess — 47
11. The Key to Redemption — 52
12. The Blackened Mountains — 58
13. The Ruthless Labyrinth — 64
14. The Echoes of Forgiveness — 70
15. The Master of Deception — 76
16. The Towering World Tree — 81
17. The Quiet Moments — 86
18. The Shadow of Destruction — 91
19. The Tale of Victory — 97

Foreword

As I take up the pen to chart the path of Brunhilde's journey in this book, 'Brunhilde: Redemption', I find myself reflecting on my lifelong fascination with her story. From my first encounter with her narrative in the echoing halls of Norse mythology, I was captivated by her larger-than-life persona that spoke volumes of courage, passion, and a paradoxical vulnerability. It was a tale that was epic in its proportions and human in its implications.

Mythology, I have come to believe, holds a mirror to our own humanity. Through its grand narratives and tragic heroines, we confront our own triumphs and failures, our dreams and despairs, our virtues and vices. And Brunhilde, a figure of indomitable strength and poignant vulnerability, is no exception.

Over the years, Brunhilde's character lodged herself into my mind, both as a formidable Valkyrie and as a woman with a heart burdened by guilt and remorse. The more I explored her tale, the more I realized that there was a profound untold story nested within the rich tapestry of Norse mythology - a story of redemption, of rising from the ashes of past mistakes, of reclaiming one's honor amidst the echoes of regret. And this, I knew, was a narrative I was compelled to tell.

Brunhilde's saga is one of tragic love, betrayal, and sacrifice, but it's also a tale of resilience, courage, and the power of forgiveness. While the lore had painted her as a tragic heroine, I saw the potential to delve deeper and explore her as a symbol of redemption, a beacon of hope that could resonate with every soul that has grappled with the inner turmoil of regret and the yearning for absolution.

'Brunhilde: Redemption' is my humble endeavor to weave this intricate tapestry of a story. It is a narrative that is rooted in mythology, yet transcends it to connect with the universal human journey. It reflects the struggle to rise from the shadows of our past, the relentless pursuit of redemption, and the eventual victory of the spirit.

In this retelling, you will journey with Brunhilde through her battles, witness her confrontation with her inner demons, and join her on her quest for redemption. You will walk with her as she retraces her steps from the past, not to dwell in them, but to learn, to grow, and to eventually rise above them.

Writing this novel has been a deeply personal journey for me, a quest of exploration and understanding. And it is my sincerest hope that as you turn the pages of 'Brunhilde: Redemption', you will not just read a tale of the ancient Norse world, but you will also experience a journey of self-discovery, of courage, and of the ultimate triumph of the human spirit over its failings.

Every echo in history holds a tale, and this is Brunhilde's. I invite you to listen, to understand, and to resonate with her journey towards redemption. May her echoes inspire you, as they have inspired me.

Welcome to 'Brunhilde: Redemption'. Let the journey begin.

1

The Isle of Forgotten Heroes

The winds howled their mournful dirge as I stood on the precipice of this forsaken isle, a monument to long-lost glory and vanished heroes. This was my sanctuary now - my penance and my prison. They called it the Isle of Forgotten Heroes, a place where echoes of the past speak louder than words ever could. This was where I had chosen to atone for my past, among the crumbling relics of forgotten wars and the skeletal remains of warriors who, like me, once reveled in the dance of power and pride.

The relentless northern gusts whipped against my weathered skin, a cold reminder of the isolation that cloaked this barren island. I heard it in the crashing of the icy waves against the jagged cliffs, each surged a symphony of remorse. I saw it in the ashen skies that mirror the tumult within my heart. Each lightning flash, each thunder's roar, they resonated with the turmoil of my guilt, a guilt that was gnawed at the corners of my being since that fateful massacre in Etzel's hall, when the once mighty and proud kingdom of the Burgundians had been brought to ruin by a vengeful violence.

My dwelling, a grim cave at the foot of the island's highest peak, offered scant comfort. Its walls, etched with my past, were the canvas of my solitude, the diary of my repentance. Within these shadows, the echoes of my deeds, and the haunting specters of my guilt found their voice, whispering tales of a time when honor had been my compass, and vengeance my misguided path.

Each day, as the sun rises, it painted the crumbled monuments in hues of gold and crimson, an ironic display of vibrant life in a place of death. And with each setting sun, the specters of my past rose, reminding me of the lives lost, the bonds broken, and the love betrayed.

I had been once a Valkyrie, a chooser of the slain, untouched by the petty conflicts of mortals. Then, I had became a queen, a pawn in a game of power and deceit, blinded by love and honor. Now, stripped of my divine status, I was but a woman, haunted by her past, desperately seeking redemption in a world that had moved on, leaving me, and this isle, forgotten.

Yet, it seemed like destiny had rolled its dice again.

One dew-kissed morning, as the first rays of the sun pierced the iron-clad skies, the bleak landscape transformed into an artist's palette. The world was bathed in hues of muted gold and blood-red, the spectral illumination casting long, contorted shadows across the barren expanse of the island. As if entranced, I found myself irresistibly drawn towards the skeletal ruins at the island's heart.

Their ancient stones, worn smooth by the relentless gnawing of time and weather, stood as silent sentinels amidst the desolation. Their time-weathered forms, etched with scars and fractures, bore testament to forgotten battles and untold stories. There, cradled in the embrace of wind-swept sand, its grains dancing a solemn waltz around it, I found the object of my fascination — an ancient stone tablet.

Its visage, hardened by age, was etched with mysterious runes, their intricate patterns partially hidden beneath a cloak of centuries-old erosion. Their convoluted patterns fascinated me, each mark a testament to an era long gone. I let my fingers trace their intricate outlines, the rough texture of the stone cold and unyielding beneath my touch. It seemed as if they whispered stories, ancient and sacred, to the rhythm of my heartbeat.

As days morphed into nights and nights gave way to days, I found myself engrossed in the riddle before me. Illuminated by the flickering glow of the fire, I poured over ancient texts, whispering forgotten prayers to the ethereal gods of old. Each deciphered symbol, each unraveled word, pulled back the veil of obscurity a little more, until the chilling prophecy revealed itself. It spoke of Fafnir, a name that froze the marrow in my bones — an entity of consuming darkness, foretold to drown the world in a torrent of chaos.

The mere whisper of the prophecy sent a shiver coursing down my spine. It wasn't fear that knotted my insides, but an understanding, bone-deep and dreadful. Fafnir, the impending doom, the harvester of despair, was destined to shroud the world in his nightmarish embrace. The prophecy was a silent scream, a desperate plea echoing through the annals of time for a savior to rise against the impending darkness.

And who was I to answer this call? A Valkyrie stripped of her wings, a queen robbed of her throne, an exile chained to her guilt. In the silence of the island, beneath the watchful gaze of a million stars, I held the tablet close, its weight heavier than any weapon I'd wielded. The wind whispered through the ruins, carrying with it the ghosts of heroes past. Their spectral eyes seemed to fix on me, an unspoken question hanging in the air.

The ghostly echoes of the prophecy still lingered in the air, a grim sonnet in the silence of the island, when a shudder ran through the island, the earth beneath my feet rumbling in apprehension. It was as if the world itself was bracing for an attack.

The heavens above, once a peaceful tapestry of cobalt blue, morphed into a tempestuous swirl of angry greys. A gust of wind howled through the ruins, carrying with it an unnerving chill. I could taste it in the air, feel it prickling my skin — the impending clash between the darkness and the last vestiges of my solitude.

The quiet was shattered by an unsettling shriek. A smoky, shapeless form appeared at the outskirts of my vision, swiftly followed by another, then another, until they were a seething mass of darkness. Minions of Fafnir. Their monstrous forms, part shadow, part nightmare, oozed malevolence, their mere presence tainting the sanctuary I had sought to create.

I was confused. Did they come to destroy me, or to lure me out of my hiding? Steeling myself, I seized my golden spear, its familiar weight a comfort in my grasp. As the first creature lunged at me, I parried its assault, the clash of our forces sending echoes through the silence of the isle. Each movement was a dance I knew all too well — the parry and thrust, the spin and slice — a deadly ballet I had been trained in since birth.

I fought with all the strength and tenacity I possessed. For each creature that fell, another took its place, their numbers seemingly endless. Each thrust of my spear, each defeated enemy, fueled my resolve, the intensity of the battle driving away any lingering doubts. I was a Valkyrie once, and I would not be defeated.

I destroyed them all. But, as the last creature dissolved into a cloud of dissipating darkness, I found myself panting, my limbs heavy. A painful clarity washed over me. My secluded sanctuary, the Isle of Forgotten Heroes, was not immune to the spreading darkness. I was no longer a solitary exile, hidden away from the world's troubles. The fight had found its way to my doorstep, and the question I had been wrestling with had now found its answer.

As I stood there, amidst the ruins of my sanctuary, I knew I had a choice to make. I could continue to live in the shadow of my past mistakes, hidden away from the world, or I could step into the light, face the darkness, and fight. The fallen valkyrie, the disgraced queen, the recluse — I could no longer be these things. There was a role I had to play, a destiny I could no longer ignore. And so, I made my decision.

2

The Serpent of the North Sea

The process of preparing the boat was a balm to my restless mind. The pull of the sail, the groan of the wooden boards under my feet, the rhythmic lapping of water against the hull — each sound, each sensation was a tether, grounding me to the present, to the task at hand.

Once the boat was ready, I looked back at what I was leaving behind. The silhouette of the island, my haven for so long, stood stoic against the backdrop of the setting sun. The Isle of Forgotten Heroes, a constant in my life of turmoil, was now a speck on the horizon. The sight tugged at something deep within me, a mix of apprehension and nostalgia, yet underlying it was a sense of resolve.

With a final glance at the receding island, I turned my gaze towards the vast expanse of the sea stretching before me. The undulating waves shimmered under the dying sunlight, a canvas of unknown possibilities. This was the start of a new chapter, a step into uncharted territories. A shiver of anticipation ran through me, the cool wind carrying whispers of what lay ahead.

My quest for redemption had begun. The journey promised

to be fraught with trials and tribulations, with battles yet to be fought, alliances to be made, and my past to be confronted. But I was ready. I wished.

From the moment the isle faded into the distance, I had braced myself for the uncertainties would throw my way. The North Sea impenetrable gray waters and foreboding skies had always been harbingers of the mysteries and dangers it concealed. But nothing could have prepared me for the monstrous entity that stirred from its slumber beneath the surface.

I was on the deck, my eyes trained on the vast expanse of water ahead, when I felt a shift, a chilling unease creeping up my spine. The sea around us began to churn violently, waves towering above the boat, threatening to engulf us. And then, it appeared. The sea serpent, a spawn of Jörmungandr, rose from the depths. Its colossal form, draped in scales of sickly green, spiraled around us, dwarfing my boat with its enormity. Its eyes, radiating a fiery red glow, fixed on me, its fangs bared ominously. A grim greeting from the sea.

As the sea serpent lunged with a force that seemed to shake the very essence of the stormy sea, its venomous fangs illuminated with a ghastly luminescence, I readied myself. Its colossal jaws aimed for my modest boat, threatening to rip through the wooden fortress that separated me from the frosty ocean depths. I held fast to my resolve, my hands tightened around the rudder, my knuckles growing white. With a sharp tug, I steered the boat clear from the gnashing jaws of the beast. The boat protested against the swift maneuver, the hull grazing against the serpent's rough scales.

The battle was underway. This was not a mere test of physical prowess and resilience. It was an assessment of the spirit, an examination of my courage, my determination. The sea serpent manifested my internal doubts and fears – the physical embodiment of the heavy price I had to pay for my past decisions. But I was ready to pay that price. I was ready to rise to the challenges of my quest, for I had elected this path, and I would follow it until the very end.

But, as the serpent gathered itself for another assault, the salty wind wrapping around me in a furious dance, I felt my courage falter. The overwhelming size of my opponent, the unyielding force of nature that was the sea serpent, seemed to swallow my spirit. My energy was waning, my resolution wavering. In a fleeting moment, I questioned if this would be my end.

Then, an ethereal presence breached my focus as a silhouette started to materialize on the water's surface. It shimmered against the ominous horizon, taking the form of a woman. She was cloaked in the spectral hues of the sea, a spectral manifestation of the ocean itself. Sigrun, the Spirit of the Sea. I had heard tales of her existence, a powerful and benign entity ruling over the sea. Yet, I hadn't fathomed our paths would cross in this lifetime.

"Sigrun," I murmured, awe creeping into my voice.

"Brunhilde," her voice responded, a harmonious blend with the rhythm of the waves, the distant cries of the seagulls, and the relentless whistle of the wind. "You fight bravely but blindly. Do you wish to know the weakness of your foe?"

"Tell me," I urged.

"The serpent, spawn of Jörmungandr, its strength lies in its aggression, but also its folly," she began. "Its eyes, they are its vulnerability. Strike true when it lunges, and you shall prevail."

The revelation startled me. How had I not seen it? The serpent's eyes – so focused on its prey and filled with raw, unguarded ferocity. It was a crucial piece of knowledge, and it tilted the scales of the battle in my favor.

"I..." I started, but the words stuck in my throat. Gratitude welled within me, but time was not on my side. The serpent was pulling back, its massive form recoiling for another strike. I settled for a nod of acknowledgment, my gaze meeting Sigrun's shimmering form one last time before turning my attention back to the imminent danger.

Before me was a monster that needed slaying, a battle demanding victory, and a destiny patiently waiting for fulfillment. Thus, armed with newfound knowledge and reinvigorated resolve, I faced the monstrous sea serpent, squaring my shoulders and steadying my grip on the rudder, ready to meet the next onslaught.

The sea roiled beneath us, a chaotic symphony of crashing waves and the serpent's thrashing coils. The beast lunged time and again, its cavernous maw snapping with a ferocity that made the very heavens shudder. Yet each time, I dodged its strikes, my boat veering this way and that in a perilous dance of survival. The battle tested my physical strength and my willpower, pushing me to my very limits.

Every muscle in my body screamed in protest, fatigue sinking its claws deeper into me with every passing moment. My grip on the rudder was shaky, my arms heavy as if wrought from iron. Yet, the adrenaline coursing through my veins, the roar of the beast, the spirit of the battle, kept me on my feet, kept me fighting. The serpent's furious onslaughts did nothing to deter my resolve; instead, they steeled my determination. I could not - would not - be defeated.

The serpent lunged again, its monstrous form a shadow eclipsing the horizon. My heart pounded in my chest, each beat echoing Sigrun's words. 'Its eyes, they are its vulnerability.

Strike true when it lunges.'

Summoning the last vestiges of my strength, I veered the boat just as the beast lunged, narrowly avoiding its gnashing teeth. In the same breath, I drew back my arm and hurled my spear. The world seemed to slow as the spear arched through the air, its path illuminated by the stormy sky. It struck true, burying itself deep into the serpent's eye. The beast roared, its cry echoing across the sea, resounding through my very soul.

The massive form of the serpent thrashed one final time before it stilled, its lifeless body sinking into the depths of the sea. Silence fell, broken only by my panting breaths and the rhythmic lapping of the waves against the hull.

Exhaustion washed over me, a wave far more potent than any the sea had to offer. Yet, beneath it was a surge of triumph. I had faced my first challenge and emerged victorious.

This was but the first step on my path to redemption, a small yet significant triumph. As I slumped against the rudder, the cold sea wind whispering across my weary form, one thought crossed my mind.

'I have a world to save.'

3

The Warmth of the Mead Hall

The whispering wind and lapping waves had been my sole companions for what seemed an eternity. Days had merged into nights, and nights into days, as I navigated the vast, unforgiving expanse of the sea. Then, after what felt like an age, I spotted it — a dark smudge on the horizon that grew into the rugged, beautiful landscape of the North.

With a sense of trepidation and excitement, I disembarked onto the shore. The rugged landscape lay before me, cradled by the dense forest and the infinite sea. The village of Eirikstorp, a settlement of the Vendelings, perched on the edge of a vast fjord, its timbered structures glowing warmly in the twilight. Wisps of smoke curled up into the chilly northern sky, carrying with them the aroma of burning wood and hearty meals.

Out from the warm glow of the nearest hut emerged a woman of venerable age. Inga, the revered volva of Eirikstorp, her sharp eyes sparkling with wisdom and a dash of intrigue. Her gaze seemed to see beyond my mortal shell, delving into the depths of my soul.

"Your arrival was foretold by the runes," she said, her voice the gentle hum of a lullaby against the evening chill. "The gods are aware of your quest."

Inga's words washed over me, a soothing balm to my weary spirit. Perhaps, here in Eirikstorp, I would find more than just another chapter in my quest; I would find kinship and understanding. Over the days that followed, Inga's wisdom proved invaluable, granting me new insight into the prophecy that had set me on this path.

But not everyone in Eirikstorp welcomed the prophecy with the same acceptance. Hjalmar, the young jarl, was a man of pragmatism, more concerned with the tangible threats of rival tribes than ominous prophecies. His ice-blue eyes were skeptical, yet beneath the hardened exterior, I sensed a burning passion for his people and their land.

"So, you bring tales of impending doom," Hjalmar said, his voice bouncing off the wooden beams of the grand mead hall, his words laced with suspicion. "Yet all I see is a stranger speaking of shadows."

"I bring not just tales, Jarl Hjalmar," I responded, meeting his challenging gaze. "I bring a chance for salvation when Fafnir's darkness falls upon your land."

"Well, you could start your quest by helping me here, Valkyrie," Hjalmar said. "Yes, we know who you are. Or you were. You're not just a common stranger. But tales, you see, oftentimes just tales."

In the warm embrace of the mead hall, with shadows pirouetting around the flame-lit room, Inga's gaze flickered between Hjalmar and me, her tone steady as the tide, "Hjalmar, we must heed the rumors of the north. A Dwarven kingdom is said to be besieged by Fafnir's minions."

A silence fell upon us, a shroud of unease. Hjalmar's grip on his mead cup tightened. He stared into its golden depths, lost in thought. A few tense moments passed before he looked up, his gaze steady and dismissive. "Rumors, Inga. Just rumors. Our reality is the impending threat of the Skjoldungs."

I could see the rationale behind Hjalmar's standpoint, the pragmatic need to address immediate threats. Yet, I also felt Inga's words resonating within me, echoing the prophecy I was meant to fulfill.

"But Hjalmar, these are not mere rumors. The prophecy," Inga's eyes met mine, their depths filled with a kind of certainty that sent a shiver down my spine, "Brunhilde is part of it. She must go north. And we must help her."

The words hung heavily in the air, a challenge and a plea intertwined. Hjalmar, however, was not easily swayed. "Brunhilde's words of doom and prophecy might mean nothing when Skjoldung blades are at our gates. She needs to prove her worth, here, with us, before I help her."

The tension in the room was palpable, like the taut string of a longbow, threatening to eclipse the harmony of the minstrel's lyre playing softly in the background. I looked at the young jarl.

"I have no desire to partake in your wars, Hjalmar," I said, my voice steady. "Mortal wars have cost me dearly in the past, the memories still etch painful reminders in my mind. I can't risk repeating the same mistakes, causing the same destruction."

Hjalmar looked at me, his stern gaze softening, replaced with a level of understanding I had not expected. The firelight danced in his eyes, revealing layers of complexity behind his hardened exterior. Here was a man molded by the responsibility he bore, a leader who carried the weight of his people's survival upon his shoulders.

"Perhaps," he started, weighing his words carefully, "we

could strike a compromise."

I raised an eyebrow at his proposal, intrigued despite my initial skepticism. Hjalmar, noticing my curiosity, continued. "If you stay here, in Eiriktorp, for a few days, to lend your strength in case the Skjoldungs attack, I will pledge my best warriors to accompany you North, to this Dwarven kingdom you seek."

His words hung in the air, a tempting offer that promised to serve both our interests. I could see the sincerity in his eyes, hear the truth in his voice. This wasn't a deception, but a desperate plea for my help, for the safety of his tribe. The dread of the war to come was palpable, the looming threat of the Skjoldungs casting a long shadow over his proud visage.

I stared into the flickering flames of the hearth, my thoughts a whirlpool of indecision. Could I risk being drawn into another conflict, open myself to the potential pain and guilt that might follow? Yet, could I turn my back on a people who might need my help, especially when their leader was willing to assist me in my quest?

In the heart of Hjalmar's mead hall, amidst the murmurs of warriors and the soft strains of a minstrel's lyre, I found myself standing on the precipice of a crucial decision. The path to redemption was never meant to be easy, and as I weighed Hjalmar's proposal, I knew, with a sinking certainty, that my trials were far from over.

"Inga, your counsel has been invaluable to me," I began, acknowledging the wise volva. "And Hjalmar, your offer is generous." My gaze found the jarl's, the firelight casting alternating shadows and light across his waiting expression. "But, my destiny lies to the North, in the prophecy that binds me."

Hjalmar stiffened, his gaze hardening. But I held up a hand to forestall his protests. "I will stay," I offered, "but only for a few days. Should the Skjoldungs not strike within that time, I must continue my quest."

The hall was quiet, the only sound the crackling of the hearth fire. Every eye was trained on Hjalmar, waiting for his reaction. The jarl was silent, his eyes locked with mine in a silent battle of wills. Then, just as the tension reached its peak, he nodded.

"A few days," he echoed, the rough edge to his voice revealing the magnitude of his concession. "And in return, if we were survive from the Skjoldungs' attack, my warriors will aid you in your quest."

The agreement was settled, sealed in the quiet warmth of the mead hall. I had not sought this complication, this entanglement in their tribal disputes. Yet, it seemed an unavoidable detour on my path to redemption.

As the jarl's warriors raised their horns in celebration, I found myself gazing into the flames of the hearth, the dance of fire and shadow reflecting the complexities of the path ahead.

4

The Weight of Our Choices

Eirikstorp felt like a taut bowstring ready to snap. Each passing day brought an increasing edge of dread, the air ripe with it. The once jovial taverns now echoed with anxious whispers, the promise of the Skjoldungs' attack casting long shadows across the faces of Vendelings. Despite the villagers' best efforts to carry on as usual, I could see the fear in their eyes; the very real possibility of losing a battle that hadn't yet begun was a constant specter.

Hjalmar, the village's young jarl, was the eye of this storm. His ironclad exterior remained unchanged, a stoic testament to his role. Yet, as we walked through the village, checking fortifications and rallying our people, I could see the burden etched deep in his gaze. He was a youth forced into a role beyond his years, and every day he bore the weight of his people's survival.

I quickly found myself drawn into this maelstrom. After only a few days, I was no longer an outsider but a part of this community. As we prepared for the impending assault, I shared my hard-earned knowledge of battle, of survival. The villagers hung onto my every word, their faces reflecting a blend of hope and fear. Word of my past deeds had spread through Eirikstorp like wildfire, my reputation as a Valkyrie transforming me into a beacon, a beacon that shone defiantly against the approaching darkness.

Among the faces looking up to me was Astrid, a young shield-maiden whose spirit was as fiery as her hair. There was an eagerness in her eyes, a thirst for knowledge that reminded me of myself when I first stepped onto the battlefield. Perhaps, under my guidance, Astrid could flourish, and her raw courage and tenacity would molding into a formidable warrior.

Training Astrid sparked a chain reaction within me. It rekindled a sense of purpose that I had almost forgotten in the midst of my prophecy and the looming battle. It was a reminder of why I had become a Valkyrie in the first place: to protect, to guide, to inspire.

Eirikstorp was not just a stop in my journey, it was becoming a part of my story. As I looked upon Astrid's determined face and Hjalmar's silent resilience, I found my resolve strengthening. I would do everything in my power to protect them from the storm that was about to descend upon us. This people had accepted me as their own. The villagers of Eirikstorp, my people now, deserved nothing less.

And yet, there was always an undertone of transience. A silent reminder that my time in Eirikstorp was finite, that I was a Valkyrie on a mission. As much as I was becoming a part of their world, I was also, inevitably, a part of another prophecy, another war. It was a delicate balancing act, one that was shattered when the Skjoldungs descended upon us.

The Skjoldungs' attack came like a tempest, sudden and brutal. Olaf, their merciless leader, led the charge. The once peaceful village of Eirikstorp was transformed into a gruesome battlefield. The rustic peace was torn apart by the screams of warriors and the clash of steel. The tranquil meadows were replaced by a maelstrom of chaos and bloodshed, the stark reality of tribal warfare staining the once green fields of Eirikstorp.

Thrust into the heart of the fray, I fought with a ferocity born out of a newfound sense of allegiance. Every thrust of my spear, every shield I raised, was not just for my prophecy, but for the people and the place I had unexpectedly grown to care for. Eirikstorp was more than just a stop in my journey. It was a place I was willing to fight for, to protect.

Under the cold gaze of the evening star, amidst the roar of the battle, I found myself questioning the prophecy. What did it mean in the face of the immediacy of war, of lives hanging in the balance? The question was as unsettling as the battle around me.

In the deathly quiet aftermath of the battle, as the dust settled and the Skjoldungs' retreat echoed in the distance, a fresh predicament confronted me. It was a victory, yes, but a victory tinged with the somber realization of the cost. The faces of the villagers, worn and bloodied but determined, resonated with a certain valor I hadn't anticipated. My connection to these people, to Eirikstorp, had somehow deepened, burrowing its way into a part of my heart.

Hjalmar and Astrid, both wounded but alive, needed me. The villagers looked at me with respect and gratitude, their trust and reliance upon me apparent in their weary eyes. And yet, for each day I spent in Eirikstorp, I felt the threads of my prophecy slipping through my fingers. My destiny lay to the North, not in this village. But how could I abandon them when they needed me?

In this whirlwind of emotions and confusion, the trader Njord arrived in Eirikstorp. He was a seasoned journeyman, frequently travelling between the North and Eirikstorp. His news from the North hit me like a gust of icy wind. Fafnir's darkness was spreading further, poisoning lands, consuming lives. His words painted a grim picture that resonated with the prophecy that haunted my steps.

I remember his eyes, alight with fear and determination as he relayed his tales. "The North needs you, Brunhilde," he said, his voice hushed and urgent in the quiet of the evening. "We all do."

I lost my words. I knew I need to go north to fulfill my duty, but should I go at this moment?

Then, Inga walked with a slow grace, her cloak trailing behind her, shimmering in the first light of dawn. The crow feather talisman she wore jingled softly as she approached me, the sound rippling through the silent morning like a soothing lullaby.

"Brunhilde," she said, her voice as soft as the dew-kissed morning breeze. "You are torn."

I nodded, feeling the knot in my chest tighten. In the presence of Inga, there was no need for pretense. Her eyes, ancient and knowing, saw beyond the facades we put up, peering directly into the heart of our worries.

"You are Valkyrie, but also human. Your heart is with us, with Eirikstorp, but your destiny is in the North," she observed, her voice imbued with understanding.

Inga's counsel was sage, measured. She spoke not to sway me one way or another but to illuminate the paths before me. "Your heart and your duty are not two separate paths, Brunhilde. They are intertwined, much like your fate is with ours."

She gestured to the waking village. "We've benefited from your presence, your strength. We've stood together in the face of the Skjoldungs. That bond isn't fleeting, but enduring. Yet your prophecy isn't a burden you carry alone; it's a thread that ties us all."

Her words, while soothing, weighed heavy. I was a Valkyrie, yes. A harbinger of fate. But I was also Brunhilde, the woman who'd found a place, a purpose among the villagers. I'd become a part of their lives, and they'd become a part of mine. Was it possible to reconcile the two halves of my existence?

"Your choices," Inga continued, her gaze serious, "will not just write your destiny, Brunhilde, but ours too. Eirikstorp, the North, perhaps the wider world. Your journey is not yours alone."

Inga's words lingered, shaping my thoughts, providing me with a different perspective. I wasn't just a stranger passing through Eirikstorp. I had become a part of their community, their fight, their destiny. But my prophecy also beckoned. It was time for a decision – one that would not just shape my destiny, but also the future of those I had come to care for.

5

The Journey to the Mountain

I decided to embark on my journey towards the North, towards my destiny. Astrid, with a fire in her eyes that mirrors my determination, insisted on accompanying me. Her progression from a green shieldmaiden to a formidable warrior had been a sight to behold. I saw a reflection of my past self in her – a fierce spirit yearning to carve her own path in this world marred by chaos and conflict.

Thorkel, Hjalmar's grizzled advisor, volunteered as well, a surprising gesture from a man who once regarded my prophecy with skepticism. His hardened gaze held a newfound respect for me. His decision, I understand, stemmed not from a sudden faith in the prophecy, but the unwavering faith in his jarl's choice to trust me. His experience and knowledge of the North would be invaluable.

As the dawn painted the horizon with its rosy hue, we set forth on our quest. The road was fraught with danger – treacherous terrains, hostile tribes, and fearsome creatures of lore that lurk in the shadows.

Thorkel, with his grizzled exterior and years of battle-wrought wisdom, quickly took the reins as our guide. His deep understanding of the land and its inhabitants proved invaluable in navigating the untamed wilderness. His stories of past wars and legends also served to lighten the mood during the harsh journey, helping us bond as a unit.

Our journey took us through the frozen tundra of Niflheim, the eerie silence of the towering Alfheim forests, and the desolate plains of Midgard. Each day brought new challenges and learnings. We encounter wild beasts, survive elemental fury, and fend off skirmishes with hostile tribes.

Our ultimate destination, the Dwarven Kingdom, lay hidden deep within the snow-capped mountains of the North. Known for their prowess in smithing and their potent ale, the dwarves were a formidable race. They were also a secretive lot, preferring to remain isolated from the wider world. Gaining their trust and cooperation will be a significant challenge.

Fafnir's darkness loomed over the Dwarven Kingdom. His minions lay siege to their stronghold, hoping to harness the dwarves' legendary smithing skills for their dark lord's nefarious plans. The once-thriving kingdom now teetered on the brink of collapse, its future precariously balanced on the edge of a knife.

The minions were creatures of shadow and malice, a stark contrast to the proud and sturdy dwarves. Their form seemed fluid, darkness coalescing into fearsome shapes, their eyes burning with an unholy green flame. They moved with an unnatural agility, their bodies undulating and merging with the shadows, making it difficult to anticipate their movements. Some were as tall as men, while others were hulking beasts. Despite their varying forms, one thing was consistent – their sheer malevolence, the palpable aura of dread they radiated.

Durin's Hold, the stronghold under siege, was nestled in the heart of a towering mountain range. Its stone walls blended seamlessly with the craggy surroundings, the fortifications a testament to the dwarves' architectural prowess. Yet, these once impregnable defenses were now under relentless assault. The minions seemed to come in endless waves, clawing and battering at the stronghold's gates, their shrieks echoing off the stone ramparts. The stronghold's mighty catapults and crossbows fought back, launching volleys of flaming projectiles into the sea of writhing shadows. Yet, each fallen minion seemed to be replaced by two more, the siege an ever-escalating nightmare.

Getting inside the stronghold amidst the siege was a daunting task. After observing the stronghold from a safe distance, we noticed a pattern to the minions' assault – their waves seemed to ebb momentarily after each intense assault, likely regrouping before the next. It was during one of these brief lulls that we decided to make our move. Using the distraction provided by the stronghold's defenses and under the cover of the ensuing chaos, we raced across the no man's land that separated us from the stronghold. It was a harrowing dash, the roar of battle and the heat of the catapult fire making the journey all the more perilous. However, we were able to reach the stronghold's gates.

The walls of Durin's Hold rose before us, a formidable fortress of stone and steel nestled within the heart of the mountain range. As we approached the guarded gate, the air buzzed with tension, the beleaguered city resonating with a disquieting undercurrent of despair.

The Dwarven guards narrowed their eyes at us, suspicion etched into their stern faces. Their weariness was evident in the set of their shoulders, the grime of battle staining their armors, and the grim determination in their eyes. They bore the scars of Fafnir's siege – a siege that had transformed their once thriving city into a battleground.

"We've no need for outsiders," one of the guards growled, his voice gravelly and fatigued, as he crossed his axe in front of the gateway, barring our path.

Behind him, the stronghold bristled with activity. Dwarven warriors rushed about, fortifying their positions, their faces etched with stoicism as they prepared for the next wave of Fafnir's minions. The stronghold, I noted, was far from defeated. But the relentless onslaught had taken its toll.

Astrid stepped forward, her gaze meeting the guard's with a defiant spark. "We're not here to cause trouble," she stated, her tone firm. "We're here to help."

A moment of silence passed before the guard grunted, his gaze flitting between us. "We've heard such promises before from humans," he retorted, his mistrust palpable. "How can we trust that you won't turn on us when things get tough?"

It was Thorkel who spoke next, his voice steady and resolute. "We know what you're up against. We are here to lend our strength to your cause."

The guard's gaze hardened as he scanned Thorkel, as if trying to discern the truth in his words. It was an uphill battle, I realized, to gain their trust. But we had to try. The fate of Eirikstorp, the North, and even the wider world hinged on this.

I stepped forward, meeting the guard's eyes. "I am Brunhilde," I stated. "A Valkyrie. My path led me here, to aid in your fight against Fafnir. I give you my word, we stand with you."

The silence that followed was deafening. The guard's gaze bore into mine, his eyes searching, weighing my words. I returned his stare, hoping he'd see the sincerity in my eyes.

The Dwarven Kingdom's survival was not just their fight, but ours too.

Finally, after what felt like an eternity, the guard lowered his axe. "Very well, Valkyrie," he said, his voice low and grudgingly respectful. "Welcome to Durin's Hold. May your stay be... fortuitous."

As we stepped through the city's gates, I knew the real battle was only beginning. Fafnir's darkness was spreading, and we were in the heart of it now. But we were not alone. We had allies, and together, we would face whatever came our way.

"Fortuitous," I mused, the word echoing in my mind. Yes, it was an appropriate wish. Fortuitous for Durin's Hold, for Eirikstorp, for all of us. For our journey was not just mine, but intertwined with those I had come to care for. And in this grim, besieged city, we would find a way to stand together, against the spreading shadow.

6

The Heart of the Stronghold

Within the stone confines of Durin's Hold, Thorkel's reputation as a seasoned warrior and my identity as a Valkyrie held weight. We navigated the bustling, anxious city, eventually finding ourselves before the opulent doors of King Eitri's hall.

The grandeur of the chamber was humbling, a testament to the might and glory of the Dwarven Kingdom. Golden threads wove through the stone columns, shimmering in the torchlight, as sculptures of valiant Dwarven warriors loomed overhead. At the far end of the hall, on a raised dais sat King Eitri, an imposing figure amidst a crowd of advisors.

King Eitri was a leader sculpted by adversity. His once dark beard now streaked with grey, his eyes glinted with a sharp intelligence that belied his age. His gaze was penetrating, scrutinizing us as we approached, gauging the threat or potential we presented.

Thorkel stepped forward first, his voice echoing through the grandeur of the chamber. "King Eitri, we come to you as allies in the battle against Fafnir. We ask for your trust and an opportunity to lend our strength to your cause."

King Eitri's gaze moved from Thorkel to me, his eyes narrowing slightly. "You claim to be a Valkyrie," he said, his voice a low rumble. "Do you expect me to entrust the fate of my people to a prophecy and its harbinger?"

My heartbeat echoed in my ears as I met his gaze. I saw the weight of his worry, the burden of his people's survival on his shoulders. He was a king on the precipice, trying to safeguard his kingdom from the spreading darkness.

"I do not ask for blind faith, King Eitri," I responded, my voice steady. "Only for a chance to prove our worth. I have faced Fafnir's minions in my past, and I understand the threat they pose. Your people have fought valiantly, and when the time is right, together we can turn the tide."

A heavy silence descended upon the hall. I could feel the weight of his scrutiny, the anticipation hanging in the air as King Eitri contemplated my words.

He leaned back in his throne, stroking his beard pensively. "Very well," he conceded, his gaze hard but thoughtful. "I will grant you this opportunity. Show us your worth, Valkyrie. Prove that your allegiance to our cause is not merely words."

A sense of resolve washed over me. It was a small victory, but a crucial one. King Eitri's cautious optimism had cracked the door open for us.

"We won't let you down, King Eitri," I vowed, my gaze focused on the task ahead. Durin's Hold was not merely a stop on my journey. It was a beacon of hope in a world shadowed by Fafnir's darkness. And I would do everything in my power to keep that beacon alight.

The king introduced us to his advisor, Kjaran, a grizzled veteran who carried an air of rugged authority. His hair and beard were a wild mane of silver, eyes glinting with wisdom and battle-hardened resolve.

Kjaran invited us to delve deeper inside the stronghold. "Your mission to defeat the darkness, I think, lies within the Dwarven Vault," he announced, leading us through the winding stone passages. His voice echoed ominously against the ancient walls, "Within its confines reside the remnants of our ancient knowledge and artifacts of immeasurable power."

The weapon I should seek, as he detailed, was an ancient one - 'Gungnir's Echo'. The mere mention of the name stirred a sense of awe in the chamber. It was a weapon of legend, whispered in hushed tones, revered in the ancient Dwarven lore. A weapon believed to hold the power to vanquish Fafnir.

Yet, as we soon discovered, our quest wasn't as straightforward. The Vault was locked, guarded by a riddle that had baffled even the brightest Dwarven minds. As I stood before the massive stone door, engraved with the riddle in Dwarven runes, I felt a rush of anticipation mixed with anxiety. Here was a challenge that merged brute force and keen intellect - a true test of my Valkyrie mettle.

It was then I noticed the other Dwarf in the room, Ivaldi. A Dwarf unlike any I had met. He was unassuming, almost overlooked amidst the grizzled warriors, yet his eyes held a spark of curiosity. I could see he was not a warrior, but a scholar, a keeper of Dwarven history and lore.

Seeing my interest, Ivaldi ventured to meet me, his parchment-filled satchel bouncing against his side. "It's a conundrum," he said to me, his gaze intent on the vault door. "But perhaps, with your ancient knowledge and my understanding of Dwarven history, we might unravel it."

Thus began our delve into the depths of Dwarven lore, our

days filled with dusty tomes and heated debates. From the very moment I set my eyes on the ancient manuscripts and historical accounts of the Dwarven Kingdom, I was entranced. We began our scholarly journey into the heart of Dwarven lore, a world teeming with tales of valor, extraordinary craft, and ancient wisdom. The pages were a testament to their indomitable spirit, their resilience reverberating through every letter, every story, every piece of their fascinating history.

The Dwarves, I came to learn, were not just miners and smiths as I'd first believed. They were inventors, scholars, guardians of knowledge, protectors of the natural balance. Their civilization was steeped in respect for the earth's resources, wisdom won from the heart of the mountains they called home.

One tale, in particular, stood out. It was the story of Gungnir's Echo, the legendary weapon our quest was centered upon. The lore spoke of the first Dwarven king, Durin, who was gifted an echo of Odin's spear Gungnir by the god himself. Durin used it to establish peace and prosperity, but understanding its immense power, he chose to lock it away. He devised a riddle, a test of wisdom and valor, ensuring only a worthy soul could retrieve it.

The riddle, transcribed in Dwarven runes on the vault door, was a complex matrix of letters and symbols. It read as follows: "Born in the heart of mountains high, carved by hands unseen. Both weapon and a home I am, in peace and war, I gleam."

Under the dim light of the ancient Dwarven lamps, Ivaldi and I would ponder over this enigma. We would debate, argue, share insights. But despite our best efforts, the answer eluded us. The riddle, much like the vault it guarded, remained silent, withholding its secrets from our desperate scrutiny.

As each day bled into the next, the sense of urgency amplified. The weight of our task was a constant reminder of the war that raged outside. We could hear the distant cries of battle, the clanging of steel, the roars of Fafnir's minions. The weapon was within our grasp, yet frustratingly out of reach. Would we decipher the riddle in time? Or would Durin's Hold fall, its legacy lost to the annals of time?

The minions' relentless onslaught escalated, the barrage pushing the steadfast Dwarven Kingdom to the brink. These beings were grotesque manifestations of Fafnir's corrupt magic, their forms warped and deformed, their scales harder than iron. Their very existence was an affront to life itself.

Even the most formidable defenses fall under the burden of incessant assault. Despite the indomitable spirit of the dwarves, the minions were gradually eroding the stronghold's walls. Their dark magic seeped into the stonework, poisoning the lifeblood of the city. A dreadful truth had dawned upon us – we were caught in a war of attrition we were steadily losing.

As the defenses weakened, morale diminished. The dwarves, once fiery and resolute, were being suffocated by the looming specter of defeat. Depletion of supplies, loss of kin, and constant conflict were draining their spirits. Despair was inching its way into their hearts, threatening to extinguish the last flickers of hope.

In the midst of this chaos, the riddle remained an unbroken fortress, repelling all our attempts to breach it. Each failure was a heavy blow, our patience wearing thin, our frustrations escalating. As the minions bore down on the city, our time was running out. I could no longer stand idle. The kingdom needed every able hand, every valiant heart. The walls were crumbling, the city was faltering, and there was only one choice left.

I must join the battle.

7

The Courage of the Dwarves

As the sun began to set, painting the sky in hues of fiery orange, Thorkel, Astrid and I found ourselves among the embattled dwarves. The clangor of swords, the thunderous crashes, the primal roars of defiance; it was a symphony of chaos. We fought with all we had, our every strike a desperate plea for survival, our every step a dance with death. Each moment of respite was as fleeting as a bird's flight through the stormy sky.

The minions of Fafnir, like an unending tide, kept crashing against our defenses. With monstrous grins and vile sneers, they sought to break our spirit, to push us into despair. But we stood firm, refusing to let their darkness consume us.

I fought alongside Thorkel, his grizzled face etched with determination. Astrid, as fierce as any seasoned warrior, slashed and parried with a fury that belied her youth. We fought until our muscles screamed for mercy and our vision blurred. With each fallen foe, our resolve hardened, our determination steeled. But exhaustion was a relentless foe, and I knew that the next wave would press us harder than ever before.

In the heat of the battle, I watched the dwarves around me. They were worn, bloodied, and beaten, but not broken. Their faces were grim, but their eyes shone with an unwavering resolve. It was then, amidst the clangor and chaos, that the answer of the riddle struck me, as clear as the first light of dawn.

The riddle said: "Born in the heart of mountains high, carved by hands unseen. Both weapon and a home I am, in peace and war, I gleam."

The dwarves had long believed this to pertain to the literal physical materials from which their weapons and homes were forged. But the answer wasn't iron or stone, as they had long thought. It wasn't something physical at all, but rather something metaphysical and deeply philosophical.

Seeing the dwarves' struggle against Fafnir's minions, their indomitable spirit, their will to defend their home at any cost, Brunhilde experienced an epiphany. The riddle did not speak of a substance but rather a virtue, a state of being that had always defined the dwarves.

The answer was "Courage".

I moved back towards the vault, each step echoed with new-found clarity. A cheer rose up from the dwarves as I approached the vault door. "Courage!" I declared, my voice ringing out clear and strong. For a moment, all was silent. Then, with a low rumble, the door began to move, and Gungnir's Echo lay before us.

Resting on a pedestal of age-worn stone at the heart of the vault was Gungnir's Echo. It was a staff, about the height of a tall man, made from what looked like darkened, ancient oak. But despite its seemingly simple composition, a sense of awe-inspiring power radiated from it, pulsing in the air like a silent drumbeat.

The top of the staff was adorned with a multifaceted crystal, as blue as the heart of a glacier, yet its interior seemed to hold an entire cosmos, with celestial lights twinkling deep within it. The crystal was set within an ornate structure of intricate metalwork. The designs were unmistakably Dwarven - strong geometric patterns imbued with the flowing grace of nature, wrought in an alloy that glowed with an otherworldly light.

Towards the base of the staff was an array of intricate runic inscriptions, pulsating with a soft luminescence, their ancient language telling a tale of legendary battles, valorous heroes, and promises of protection to those who wielded it with justice and courage.

Holding Gungnir's Echo in my hand was like grasping the heartbeat of the world itself. It vibrated softly, pulsing with an energy that felt ancient and yet undeniably alive. It was a weapon of undeniable power, forged in the crucible of Dwarven ingenuity and imbued with the might of their ancestral heroes. Despite its formidable power, Gungnir's Echo had an elegance about it, a harmony that sang of balance and unity.

It was not just a weapon. Gungnir's Echo was a beacon of hope, a symbol of resistance against the ever-looming darkness. It was a testament to the indomitable spirit of the Dwarves, a testament to their unyielding courage in the face of despair.

Even so, I still couldn't understand how much power this weapon could unleash, and whether my body would be able to withstand it. One thing was certain, the dwarves, even including King Eitri, did not dare to use it at this time. I was the one who had to do this.

As they came again, I must be ready. The final wave bore down on us, an inky sea of malevolence stretching as far as the eye could see. Thousands of Fafnir's minions - grotesque creatures born of darkness and ruin, scaled and spiked, their eyes gleaming with a ravenous hunger. I stood before them, the last bastion between the vile horde and the Dwarf kingdom I'd come to hold dear. Gungnir's Echo felt warm in my grasp, a comforting presence amidst the impending storm.

As the vile horde drew nearer, the air around me seemed to thrum with power, rippling out from Gungnir's Echo. I could feel the echoes of the Dwarven heroes of old, their valor, their indomitable spirit resonating with my own. Raising the staff high above my head, I channeled my inner strength into it, feeling its power surge in response. The staff's intricate runes glowed brighter, and the celestial lights within the crystal pulsed with an ethereal light.

And then I struck.

The ground beneath us shuddered as a wave of pure, brilliant energy surged forth from Gungnir's Echo. It tore through the charging horde like a divine tempest, sending minions flying, their wretched cries echoing eerily across the battlefield. I watched as the wave of energy swept across the minions, their forms dissolving into shadowy wisps that were swiftly swept away by the Dwarven wind.

As the last echoes of the battle faded, I stood there, panting, drained, but triumphant. Gungnir's Echo pulsed softly in my hands, its job done, its promise fulfilled. Around me, the Dwarven stronghold lay silent, save for the soft rustling of the wind and the distant cheers of the dwarves.

There was a peaceful lull that felt almost foreign. The stronghold was marked by the scars of battle, debris and ruins strewn about, the bodies of fallen minions piled high. But amidst the wreckage, there was life, the Dwarven folk moving with renewed vigor to clear the wreckage and begin their restoration.

That night, in the heart of the stronghold, a celebration was held. It was a simple affair, as befitting the dwarves' nature. Ale flowed freely, and tales of the day's victory echoed off the stone walls. I found myself beside King Eitri, a figure stooped with age but imbued with a wisdom and strength that was palpable.

"Eitri," I said, breaking the companionable silence that had fallen between us, "I must find Fafnir."

The old king's brow furrowed, his eyes far away. "The darkness that Fafnir has spread is far and wide," he said slowly. "It has poisoned our lands, claimed the lives of many. But as for where he himself lurks... I cannot say."

I nodded. The path ahead was uncertain.

"You might seek Skadi," Eitri suggested then, his voice thoughtful. "If anyone would know where to find Fafnir, it would be her."

His words sparked a new resolve within me. Skadi. The Goddess of Winter. If that was where my path led next, then that was where I would go. I thanked King Eitri, raising my mug in a salute before draining the last of my ale. Tomorrow, I would begin my journey to seek Skadi. Tonight, however, I would enjoy this moment of peace, this respite, this victory.

8

The Ghost from the Past

The icy wind whipped around me, tearing at my flowing silver hair as we pressed on through the unforgiving landscape. Tundra stretched out before us in all directions, a desolate wasteland that seemed to mirror the turmoil that roiled within my breast. Astrid strode beside me, her fiery hair and fierce green eyes a beacon of strength amidst the cold. Thorkel, grizzled and wise beyond his years, followed close behind.

"Skadi awaits," I whispered, more to myself than my companions. Hope flickered in my heart, fragile as a candle flame in the darkness. If I could find the Goddess of Winter, if I could face my past and atone for my mistakes, perhaps there was still a chance to save our world from the encroaching shadow.

As we crested a hill, a village emerged from the mists below, nestled between the jagged mountains that loomed like ancient guardians. The buildings huddled together, their timber frames and thatched roofs fending off the biting chill. Smoke rose from the chimneys, its tendrils reaching toward the leaden sky as if beseeching the heavens for mercy. The villagers moved about their daily tasks, wrapped in furs and wool, their faces weathered but etched with the determination to endure.

"Let us rest here awhile," Thorkel rumbled, his voice as deep and solid as the mountains themselves. "We will need our strength for the climb ahead."

"Very well," I acquiesced, though my heart ached to press on. We made our way down the hillside, the wind howling a mournful lament as if echoing my own anguish.

Entering the village felt like stepping into another world. The air was rich with the scents of roasting meat and baking bread, a welcome respite from the stark cold that had been our constant companion. Laughter and the clatter of tankards filled the air, the people's voices weaving a vibrant tapestry of life amidst the desolation. The villagers welcomed us with open arms, their warmth reaching out to embrace us even as the icy tendrils of the past tightened around my heart.

As we prepared for the night, the haunting melodies of the village minstrel stirred something deep within me – memories of laughter and love, of battles fought and won, but also of betrayal and loss.

The fire's warmth had begun to thaw my frozen heart when the tavern door creaked open, and a gust of cold wind tore through the room. He stood there on the threshold, his golden hair tousled by the breeze, his cerulean eyes like twin pools of moonlight. Erik Wolfsbane, they called him, though few knew the true reason behind that name. His lean build belied the strength that lay beneath, and his tunic clung to his broad shoulders like a second skin.

"Evening, friends," he greeted us with a warm smile, his voice rich and melodic like a well-tuned lute. As he approached our table, I couldn't help but be reminded of Siegfried, the man

I loved in the past. My heart clenched at the thought, and I struggled to maintain my composure.

"Good evening, Erik," Astrid replied, her voice steady despite the tension that suddenly filled the air. "Won't you join us?"

"Thank you," he said, taking a seat beside Thorkel. His gaze met mine, and for a moment, time seemed to stand still. A mixture of recognition and curiosity flickered within those blue depths, a mirror of the emotions that churned within me. The resemblance between him and Siegfried was uncanny, and I felt as though the past had come back to haunt me.

"Your journey has been a long one," he observed, his gaze never leaving mine. "I trust you have found some respite here in our humble village?"

"Indeed, we have," I answered, my voice barely above a whisper. "The kindness of your people has been a balm to our weary souls."

"Ah, then we are honored to provide what little comfort we can," he replied, his smile both gentle and genuine. "And may I ask what brings you to this remote corner of the world?"

My eyes locked with his as I answered, "We seek Skadi, the Goddess of Winter, in the hope that she might aid us in our quest."

"An ambitious undertaking," he mused, his brow furrowing slightly. "But one that is not without its dangers. The path to Skadi's domain is treacherous and fraught with peril."

"Yet it is a path we must walk," I said.

"Then I wish you luck on your journey, Brunhilde Valkyr," he said solemnly, his eyes never wavering from mine. "May the gods guide your steps and protect you from the darkness that lies ahead."

"Thank you, Erik Wolfsbane," I replied, my heart heavy with

the weight of unspoken words.

I watched him disappear into the shadows. As the fire burned low, and the music faded into silence, I closed my eyes and prayed for the courage to confront the darkness within. Erik's presence had awakened something within me – a torrent of memories and emotions I had long sought to bury deep beneath the surface.

"Are you alright, Brunhilde?" Astrid asked, her voice laced with concern. Thorkel looked at me with furrowed brows, his eyes filled with empathy.

"Forgive me," I whispered, struggling under the weight of my past. "There is much I have kept hidden from you both."

"Tell us," Thorkel urged gently. "We are here for you, as we always have been."

"Very well," I sighed, knowing that the time had come to confront the truth. The walls I had built around my heart began to crumble, giving way to the storm that raged within.

"Many years ago, I loved a man named Siegfried. He was a brave and noble warrior, much like our dear Erik," I admitted, my voice trembling with emotion. "But I betrayed him, and in doing so, I betrayed myself."

Astrid's hand found mine, offering comfort and solace as I continued my tale. "I was young and foolish, blinded by pride and ambition. My love for Siegfried was true, but I allowed jealousy and envy to poison my heart. And in the end, it led me down a path of darkness and despair."

"Is that why Erik's presence affects you so profoundly?" Thorkel inquired, his voice gentle and understanding.

"Indeed," I confessed. "For in his eyes, I see the reflection of the man I once loved – and the woman I used to be."

"Your journey for redemption is not only about saving our

world, but also about healing your own heart," Astrid said. "It is the ghosts of our past that haunt us the most – and it is only through confronting them that we can truly find peace."

"Let us help you, Brunhilde," Thorkel insisted, his hand gripping mine with fierce determination. "We are your friends, your family."

"Thank you, both of you," I whispered, my heart swelling with gratitude. "Your support means more to me than you could ever know. May the gods watch over us all."

As the night wore on, I found solace in the knowledge that I was not alone – and that together, we would confront the shadows that haunted us, and emerge stronger than before.

9

The Hope to Rise Again

The first light of dawn crept through the cracks in the wooden walls, casting a golden glow over the small room we had taken refuge in. I lay on the floor, my eyes tracing the intricate knots carved into the ceiling beams, each one entwining with another like the threads of fate that bound us together. As I listened to the steady breathing of Astrid and Thorkel, I felt the knot in my chest tighten, as if the weight of my past sins was growing heavier with each passing moment.

I got up and walked out of the room, hoping to find peace and renewed vigor in the bright morning. Outside the inn I stood looking up at the high mountains we were about to visit. But even such a beautiful sight could not calm my heart.

"Good morning, Brunhilde. Your thoughts seem troubled," a soft voice whispered, as someone came. It was Erik, his golden hair catching the sun's rays like a halo around his head. He approached me and stood by my side, his blue eyes searching mine with a mixture of concern and curiosity.

"Good morning, Erik. Did I not tell you to stay away from me?" I snapped, my voice harsher than intended. But instead of recoiling, Erik merely raised an eyebrow, his gaze never wavering.

"Perhaps I am a glutton for punishment," he replied with a wry smile. "Or perhaps I simply wish to understand the woman who has captured the hearts of so many."

"Then you shall be sorely disappointed," I retorted, bitterness seeping through my words. "For there is little worth knowing about a fallen queen and a failed Valkyrie."

"Is that what you truly believe?" Erik asked, his eyes narrowing slightly. "Or is it merely what you want others to think?"

I glared at him with all the fury of a storm-tossed sea. "Do not presume to know me, nor the depths of the darkness that lies within my heart."

"Then enlighten me," he challenged, his voice low and steady. "Tell me of your past, of the choices that have led you here – and perhaps, in doing so, you may find a measure of peace."

"Speak not to me of peace," I hissed. "For it is a luxury that I have long since forsaken."

"Then what do you hope to gain by continuing this quest?" Erik asked, his voice gentle but insistent. "Is it redemption you seek, or merely a chance to silence the demons that haunt your every step?"

"Both," I whispered, my voice barely audible even to my own ears. "I must atone for the lives I have destroyed. Perhaps, I can finally lay my own ghosts to rest."

"Then let me help you," Erik offered, his tone sincere. "Let me share in your burdens, just as Astrid and Thorkel have done – and together, we shall face whatever comes our way."

"Your kindness is wasted on me," I replied, shaking my head. "For it is not compassion I require, but strength – and the courage to confront the darkness within myself."

"Strength and courage are virtues that can be found in many forms," Erik countered, stepping closer until our faces were mere inches apart. "Even in the most unlikely of places."

"Like the heart of a stranger?" I asked, my voice tinged with disbelief.

"Sometimes," he said, his gaze locked with mine. "Especially when that stranger sees something within you that you have long since forgotten."

"And what might that be?" I questioned, my curiosity piqued despite my best efforts.

"Hope," he answered simply, his eyes shining with conviction. "The hope that even those who have fallen can rise again – and that redemption is not an elusive dream, but a reality within our grasp."

As his words echoed through my mind, I felt something stir within me – a flicker of warmth that cut through the coldness of my heart like the first rays of dawn. And as I looked into Erik's eyes, I knew that he spoke the truth – and that, perhaps, there was still hope for me yet.

"Thank you," I murmured, my voice barely audible as I allowed myself to believe, if only for a moment, in the possibility of redemption. "For reminding me."

As I stood there, I realized that the way to redemption was through atonement – not only for my past mistakes but also for the choices that led me down this path. The journey to find Skadi was more than just a quest to save my world; it was an opportunity to mend the broken pieces of my soul and reclaim the life I once knew.

I whispered, "Will you help me find Skadi and face the consequences of my actions?"

Erik hesitated for a moment, weighing the words on his tongue before he spoke. "I promise," he said, determination burning in his gaze. "We will find Skadi, and you will have your chance to atone."

"Then let us begin," I turned.

Astrid and Thorkel already had stood nearby, their expressions a mixture of concern and relief as they saw the resolve etched upon my face.

"Friends," I began, addressing them with newfound purpose. "We set forth to find Skadi today. But know this – our journey is not an easy one. We must face whatever trials lie ahead with courage and conviction."

Astrid nodded solemnly, her eyes shimmering with unshed tears. "We are with you, my queen," she murmured, her voice barely audible as she placed a comforting hand upon my shoulder.

"And so am I," Thorkel added gruffly, his stoic facade cracking ever so slightly as he offered a rare smile.

We gathered our belongings and prepared to leave the village behind. As we made our way towards the outskirts, I could feel the weight of my past lifting ever so slightly from my shoulders, replaced by the burden of responsibility that lay ahead.

As we trudged onward through the dense, fog-choked forest that blanketed the foothills of the mountain, I felt the pull of destiny tugging at my very soul. The village, with its warm hearths and simple comforts, had faded into the distance, leaving us alone with our thoughts and the silent whispers of the trees.

"Look!" Astrid exclaimed suddenly, pointing towards a break in the trees where an ancient stone path snaked its way up the mountainside. "The path to Skadi's abode."

"Good," Erik said. "We're on the right track!"

"Then let us make haste," Thorkel grumbled, his brow furrowed as he gazed up at the imposing peak that loomed above us. "Night will be upon us soon, and I'd rather not face the creatures that dwell within these woods."

"Are you alright?" Astrid asked, her eyes filled with concern as she studied my weary expression. "You've been so quiet since we left the village."

I hesitated, searching for the words to convey the turmoil that raged within me. I looked at Erik before answering. "I'm... coming to terms with the shadows of my past, Astrid." My voice barely a whisper as I stared down at the moss-covered stones beneath my feet. "But I am determined to forge a new path."

Astrid reached out, her fingers brushing against mine as she offered a small smile. "I believe in you. We all do."

"Indeed," Thorkel added gruffly, his gaze never leaving the path ahead. "We've come too far to turn back now."

Their words touched something deep within me — a spark of hope that flickered in the darkness, casting just enough light to illuminate the way forward.

"Thank you, guys," I whispered, my voice barely audible above the rustle of the wind through the trees. "For everything."

As we reached the crest of a hill, the mountain's peak came into view — a jagged, ice-shrouded monolith that pierced the heavens like a blade. It was there, amidst the eternal snows and howling winds.

Hand in hand, we pressed onward, our spirits buoyed by the knowledge that redemption lay just beyond the horizon. And as the final rays of the setting sun bathed the world in a tapestry of gold and crimson, I knew that I had found not only the strength to confront my demons but also the courage to embrace the future that awaited me. For in the end, it is not the mistakes of our past that define us, but rather the choices we make in the face of adversity – and the love and loyalty of those who stand by us when the night is darkest.

10

The Dwelling of the Goddess

The biting cold gnawed at my very bones as we approached the dwelling of Skadi, the Goddess of Winter. This arduous journey had taken its toll on us all.

"Are you sure this is the place?" asked Astrid, her short-cropped red hair dusted with frost, her breath materializing in a cloud of icy vapor. Her fierce green eyes searched the horizon for any sign of life. She was brave and young, stubbornly pushing herself to become a better warrior. It pained me to see her struggle in this unforgiving landscape, but she was driven by a fire within, seeking inspiration in my own journey .

"Skadi's dwelling lies beyond that ridge," replied Thorkel, his long white beard frozen with icicles. Decades of battle had etched deep lines onto his grizzled face. Though he was wise and experienced, he too sought redemption alongside me, grappling with past mistakes that haunted him like specters.

"Let's keep moving then," said Erik, his golden hair and bright blue eyes catching the faint light that managed to pierce the gloom of the northern sky. His resemblance to Siegfried stirred up feelings within me again, forcing me to confront the guilt that I carried like a heavy burden. He was a better man, though; not as strong as Siegfried, but kind-hearted. I was glad he was the one who accompany us, not Siegfried.

As we traversed the barren, snow-covered terrain, the wind whispered secrets to me, reminding me of my past, of my fall from grace, and of my quest for redemption. I shivered, not only from the chill air, but also from the sense of foreboding that hung heavy upon us.

The dwelling of Skadi loomed before us, a fortress of ice and stone nestled within the jagged peaks of the mountains. Its crystalline walls shimmered with an otherworldly glow as if they contained the frozen souls of countless warriors. The entrance to her abode was guarded by two massive ice sculptures, resembling wolves snarling at any who dared approach. The sight of it sent shivers down my spine, but I knew that we had come too far to turn back now.

My silver hair whipped around my face as we ascended the frostbitten steps, our boots crunching in the snow. The wind seemed to grow fiercer, urging us to reconsider our path. But I steeled myself against its warnings, for within Skadi's frigid halls lay the knowledge and power I needed to defeat Fafnir and reclaim my lost honor.

As we drew closer to the entrance, my heart raced with anticipation and dread. Would Skadi grant us her assistance? Or would she leave us to perish in the unforgiving cold, just as we had left so many others behind in our pursuit of redemption?

The ice-sculpted doors groaned as they opened before us, revealing the frozen heart of Skadi's dwelling. As we stepped inside, I was struck by the sheer scale of the cavernous chamber, its walls adorned with ancient runes, and a chill wind that seemed to carry the whispers of long-forgotten secrets.

"Welcome, travelers," said a voice that echoed like the howling of a winter storm. "I am Skadi, Goddess of Winter."

Our eyes were drawn to the figure standing before us, her presence commanding and enigmatic. Skadi's pale blue skin shimmered with frost, and her long white hair cascaded down her back, crystalline strands glistening in the dim light. Her icy blue eyes bore into us, penetrating the very depths of our souls. She wore a gown of snowflakes, each one unique and intricate, which flowed around her like a living river of ice.

"Skadi Frostborn," I breathed, feeling my knees threatening to buckle under the weight of her gaze. "We have traveled far and braved many dangers to seek your wisdom and aid."

"Indeed," she replied, her voice cold and distant. "And what is it you hope to gain from me, Brunhilde? More power? Or perhaps revenge?"

"Redemption and power," I admitted, my voice faltering. "To defeat Fafnir and reclaim my honor."

"Ah, Fafnir," Skadi mused, her eyes narrowing. "Its shadow looms large over your fate, does it not?"

I nodded, reluctant to tell her what I thought. "Kind of."

"Very well," Skadi declared, her tone resolute. "Let us see if you are worthy of my assistance."

In that moment, it felt as though the very air around us grew colder, and I sensed that we were being weighed and measured by forces beyond our comprehension. Skadi studied each of us in turn, her gaze lingering on Astrid's fierce courage, Thorkel's unwavering loyalty, and Erik's steely determination.

"Your journey has been long and arduous," Skadi observed, "and there will be more trials yet to come."

"We'll make it," I said, "Just tell us what we must do to defeat

Fafnir."

"Listen well, Brunhilde," Skadi instructed, her voice taking on a grave tone. "For the knowledge I impart unto you shall determine the course of your destiny."

As she spoke, a torrent of images and sensations flooded my mind – ancient battles, forgotten secrets, and the primal fury of the elements themselves. Through it all, Skadi's voice rang clear, providing guidance and counsel amidst the chaos.

"Now, you understand Fafnir's weakness," she said. "His power is drawn from the fears and doubts of those he seeks to dominate. Thus, to defeat him, you must conquer your own inner demons. Only then can you wield the power necessary to vanquish him."

"Where must we go?" I asked.

"Seek the heart of the Blackened Mountains," she replied, her frost-laden breath painting a vivid image upon the frosted landscape. "There, within the depths of an ancient, forgotten cavern lies Fafnir's lair. Beware, for his power is immense, and the path to his sanctum is fraught with danger. A treacherous river of molten rock flows beneath the mountains, and vile creatures born of shadow and flame lurk in the darkness, eager to claim the lives of those who dare trespass."

"Thank you, Skadi," I replied. "We will not falter in the face of these trials."

"Go forth, brave Valkyrie," Skadi intoned, her form dissipating into the swirling snows. "Face your destiny, and let the echoes of Gungnir guide you to victory."

The Goddess of Winter disappeared into the shadows, leaving us to contemplate the profound truth she had bestowed upon us. A newfound strength coursed through my veins. As we left Skadi's dwelling, the words of the ancient goddess echoing in my mind, I gazed upon the horizon and saw the ominous outline of the Blackened Mountains looming in the distance. The sight sent shivers down my spine, and I knew that the path ahead would be one fraught with danger and darkness.

"Skadi has spoken," I said, turning to my companions. "We must prepare."

Astrid nodded solemnly. "I will gather provisions and ensure our weapons are in good condition."

"I shall scout the path ahead," Thorkel rumbled, his voice like distant thunder.

"I go with you," Erik said, his piercing green eyes filled with quiet determination. I still didn't know much about him, but I believed he would prove invaluable to us.

As my companions set about their tasks, I turned my attention inward, focusing on the newfound power that coursed through my veins. The potency of Gungnir's Echo resonated within me, its presence a constant reminder of the destiny that awaited me.

In that moment, as we marched beneath the cold gaze of the stars, I felt a flicker of hope ignite within me, a bright flame that promised redemption and the chance to forge a new path for ourselves. With each step we took, that flame burned brighter, casting its light upon the shadows that sought to consume us, guiding us ever onward towards the heart of the mountain and the final confrontation that awaited us there.

11

The Key to Redemption

As I stood at the edge of a sea of grass, my eyes fixed on the distant Blackened Mountains. To get there, we would face not only the physical challenges presented by gods and mythical creatures but also the emotional and psychological burdens that weighed heavily upon us.

The first monster we faced was a giant serpent, just like I had encountered before at the sea. Its dark shape slithered through the snow, its massive form undulating beneath the frozen surface. The scales glistened like obsidian, reflecting the pale moonlight as it rose from the snow, rearing its colossal head high above us.

The serpent struck with lightning speed, its fangs glinting like daggers in the night. We dodged and parried, blades clashing against unyielding scales, but still, the creature pressed forward, relentless in its assault. Then, I realized what we needed.

"Thorkel, Erik, distract it!" I shouted. "Astrid, aim for its eyes!" We need to work as a team.

As the two men charged at the beast, drawing its attention away from me, I sprinted towards its massive body, leaping onto its sinuous form and scaling it like a living wall. The icy wind tore at my hair and clothing as I climbed higher, the serpent's writhing movements threatening to buck me off at any moment.

"Strike now!" I called out, my voice carrying on the wind as Astrid launched her arrow at the creature's vulnerable eye. The serpent roared in pain, its head thrashing wildly as it sought to dislodge me from its back. "Give it everything you've got!"

Erik and Thorkel redoubled their efforts, hacking at the monstrous snake's underbelly with desperate fury. As the creature reeled from the onslaught, I plunged my spear deep into the base of its skull. With a final, deafening shriek, the giant serpent shuddered and fell still, defeated by our combined might.

Next, we faced another giant. Or three of them. A guttural growl echoed through the trees, and the four of us froze in our tracks. From the shadows emerged a trio of trolls – hulking, twisted monstrosities with skin like granite and eyes like smoldering embers.

"Stand down!" Astrid called out, her voice strong and clear despite the fear that flickered in her eyes. "We mean you no harm. We seek only passage through these lands."

"Passage?" one troll sneered, his gravelly voice resonating with malice. "There is no safe passage here, human. Only death awaits those who trespass upon our domain."

"Then perhaps we can reach an agreement," I interjected, stepping forward. "We have no quarrel with you or your kind. Allow us to pass unharmed, and we will ensure that no harm befalls you either."

The trolls exchanged wary glances, their mistrust evident in the curl of their lips and the narrowness of their eyes. It was clear that negotiation would not come easily, but I knew that we could ill afford another battle – not when greater challenges still lay ahead.

Thorkel said, flexing his broad shoulders beneath his fur-lined cloak, "If it's incentive you need, then consider this: we have just vanquished the great serpent. Would you truly wish to test your strength against us?"

"Blasphemy!" the largest troll roared, his fury shaking the trees around us. "The serpent cannot be slain by mere mortals!"

"Yet here we stand," Erik added, gesturing towards our bloodied weapons and the unmistakable scent of serpent venom that clung to our clothes. "We have defeated one legend; do not force us to defeat another."

For a tense moment, the trolls hesitated, their stony features betraying a flicker of uncertainty. Sensing their wavering resolve, I pressed on. "Allow us this passage, and you will have our eternal gratitude. We are warriors of honor, and we swear that no harm shall come to you or your kin from our hands. This is our solemn vow."

The trolls exchanged glances once more, their eyes dark and unreadable as the shadows that clung to the forest floor. Finally, the largest among them stepped forward, his heavy footfalls shaking the earth beneath us. He rumbled, his voice like the grinding of boulders, "You may pass, but know this: if you break your vow, we shall hunt you to the ends of the earth and exact our vengeance upon you."

"Agreed," I said, inclining my head in a gesture of respect. "You have my word."

And so we passed through. Diplomacy had won the day – a victory no less significant than our triumph over the great serpent. As I gazed upon my companions, their faces etched with determination and resolve, I knew that we were capable of overcoming any obstacle, no matter how insurmountable it might seem.

We ventured deeper into the wilderness. The landscape grew ever more inhospitable, with jagged rocks and twisted roots threatening to trip us at every turn. The air was thick with menace, as though the very earth itself sought to challenge our resolve.

An unearthly screech suddenly rent the air. We looked up to see a swarm of harpies descending upon us, their talons bared and beaks clicking hungrily. They swooped down, their razor-sharp talons slashing through the air.

We unleashed a hail of arrows upon them. Our aim was true, and the deadly missiles found their mark, piercing the creatures' scaly hides and sending them plummeting lifeless to the ground.

"Take that, you foul beasts!" shouted Thorkel, his face flushed with victory.

"Stay focused!" I warned, knowing all too well the price of overconfidence. "There may be more."

"Always the voice of caution," remarked Astrid with a wry smile. "But you are right. We must remain vigilant."

We continued our arduous journey. The sun dipped low in the sky, casting warm hues of orange and gold across the landscape. We had been walking for another hours, our weary feet desperate for rest. As we turned a corner, the path led us to a secluded glade shrouded in an eerie stillness. A sense of foreboding crept up my spine, yet something compelled me to venture forward.

"Wait here," I urged my companions, feeling an inexplicable pull towards the shadows that lay ahead. Astrid, Thorkel, and Erik exchanged uncertain glances but ultimately remained behind as I continued onward alone, drawn by the whispers of fate.

The air grew colder, as if the very essence of life was being siphoned from the earth itself. And there, nestled within the heart of darkness, stood a figure born of ancient memories and forgotten dreams – an ancient seer. Her eyes were twin pools of liquid obsidian, holding within them the knowledge of countless millennia. Her voice, though soft, reverberated with the weight of untold secrets.

"Child of Valhalla," she began, her words weaving through the space between us like tendrils of smoke. "You bear the burden of guilt upon your shoulders, seeking redemption in the fires of your own making."

"Who are you?" I asked, curiosity mingling with unease.

"I am the echo of ages past, a voice carried on the winds of time. My purpose lies in guiding those who have lost their way, and you, Brunhilde, are in need of guidance."

"Tell me what I must do," I implored, desperation evident in my tone.

"Forgiveness is the key," the seer intoned, her gaze unwavering. "You must learn to forgive yourself for the sins of your past before you can truly embrace the power of redemption."

My chest tightened at her words, a storm of emotions coursing through me. How could I forgive myself when the ghosts of my past haunted every step of my journey? Yet, I sensed a truth in her message that could not be ignored.

"Forgiveness is not easily earned," I murmured, fists clenched at my sides as I struggled to reconcile the seer's wisdom with the weight of my own guilt.

"Indeed, but it is only through acknowledging your own darkness – and embracing the light within – that you can find true redemption. You have shown great courage in facing your demons, and yet you remain shackled by guilt and self-loathing.

It is not enough to merely seek redemption, young one – you must also learn to forgive yourself for the mistakes of your past."

"Can I ever truly atone for my actions?" I questioned, my voice barely a whisper amid the encroaching shadows.

"Only time will tell, child of Valhalla. But remember, the path to forgiveness begins with a single step. Redemption begins with forgiveness – both for oneself and for others."

As her final words echoed through the glade, the ancient seer vanished into the darkness from which she came, leaving behind an air of otherworldly mystery. My heart raced with trepidation and hope, for I knew that her wisdom held the key to unlocking the chains that bound me.

12

The Blackened Mountains

I stood before my companions, feeling the weight of the seer's words settle upon my shoulders like a heavy cloak. My heart pounded with a mixture of skepticism and curiosity, for the seer's message was both enlightening and daunting. Astrid, Thorkel, and Erik gazed at me expectantly, their eyes searching mine for answers.

"Forgiveness," I murmured, scoffing under my breath. "Such a simple word, yet so difficult to grasp."

"Is that what the seer spoke to you about, Brunhilde?" asked Thorkel, his unwavering voice betraying a hint of unease.

"Indeed," I replied, my skepticism laced with defiance. "She told me that forgiveness is the key to redemption – both for myself and those who walk this treacherous path beside me."

"Perhaps there is truth in her words," Erik offered cautiously, his gaze shifting between me and the others. "We have all made mistakes, after all. But we must not let them define us. Rather, we should strive to learn from them and grow stronger."

"Easy for you to say," I snapped, my chest tightening with indignation. "You have not been cast out of Valhalla, nor have you been forced to watch your loved ones suffer because of your actions."

"True," he conceded, his brow furrowing with concern. "But we have all faced our own trials and tribulations, Brunhilde. We are only human, after all – or at least, once were."

"Enough!" I barked, my fists clenched at my sides. "I refuse to be coddled by platitudes and empty promises! I will find redemption on my own terms, with or without the aid of some cryptic seer."

"Stubborn as always," Astrid murmured, shaking her head with a wry smile. "But perhaps that is what has brought us this far, my queen. Your determination and resilience have been an inspiration to us all."

"Is it really so wrong to want to right the wrongs of my past?" I asked, more to myself than to my companions. The shadows of doubt danced through my mind, taunting me with the prospect of failure.

"Of course not," Thorkel reassured me, placing a hand on my shoulder. "But we must also be willing to accept our imperfections and embrace the power of forgiveness – both for ourselves and others."

"Only by casting aside the chains of guilt," the seer's words echoed in my head, "and embracing the light within, can you find true redemption."

"Perhaps," I whispered, my voice barely audible to my friends. "Perhaps there is wisdom in her words after all."

"Then let us carry her message with us as we continue our journey," Astrid suggested, her eyes shining with renewed resolve. "For if forgiveness is the key to redemption, then surely we are all worthy of a second chance."

"Very well," I conceded, my skepticism slowly giving way to

cautious optimism. "We shall see if the power of forgiveness can truly set us free."

With newfound determination, our ragtag band of lost souls ventured forth into the unknown, each step bringing us closer to our destination.

As we ventured deeper into the unforgiving wilderness, we encountered a band of marauders who sought to take advantage of our perceived vulnerability. But they underestimated us, for our unity had only grown stronger. We fought with ferocity, our blades and arrows singing through the air as we defended ourselves against the vicious onslaught. My old instincts took over, the desire for vengeance rising within me like a tempest.

But amidst the chaos of battle, the seer's wisdom echoed in my ears: "Redemption begins with forgiveness." As I stood over the defeated marauders, my sword poised to deliver the final blow, I hesitated. Instead of slaying them, I offered them mercy, on the condition that they abandon their violent ways.

"Your lives are spared," I declared, my voice firm yet compassionate. "Let this be a chance for you to forge a better path – one of honor and redemption."

We left the defeated bandits behind, and I could feel my companions' respect for my decision. We had grown not only as individuals but also as a united force. Our weary yet determined band pressed onward, bound by loyalty, courage, and the unyielding hope of salvation.

And one night, as we arrived at a secluded area, surrounded by an ethereal grove of ancient trees draped in silvery moss, we shared our burden to each other.

Astrid spoke first, her gaze locked on the ground. "I have always been haunted by the fear of not living up to my father's expectations. He was a great warrior, and I am but a shadow of his legacy."

"Your strength lies in your resilience, Astrid," I told her, touched by her vulnerability.

"Thank you, my queen." She looked up, her eyes glistening with unshed tears.

Thorkel stepped forward, his shoulders slumped in defeat. "I was cast out of my village when I failed to protect those I loved. It is a shame I cannot escape. Oftentimes, I want to die as well."

"Be strong, Thorkel," I said.

"Yes, your heart is pure," Erik reassured him. "You have shown us nothing but kindness and loyalty."

"Thank you," Thorkel whispered, his voice cracking.

Erik hesitated before sharing his own burden. "I was once a poet, celebrated for my verses. But in my arrogance, I lost sight of the beauty that inspired me. Now, I am but an echo of the man I once was."

"Your words still carry great power, Erik," Astrid said with conviction. "They inspire us all."

"Thank you," he murmured, visibly moved.

As they bared their souls, I felt the weight of my own guilt grow heavier. "I have done great wrongs in my past," I admitted, voice trembling. "Many suffered because of my actions. People hate me, as I hate myself. Can I ever be free from this anguish?"

"Only you can make that choice, Brunhilde," Thorkel responded gently. "But remember the seer's words – forgiveness is the key."

"Perhaps it is time to forgive myself," I whispered, though doubt still clung to me like chains.

"Indeed," Erik agreed. "For we are all destined for greatness, but only if we dare to embrace our flaws and seek redemption."

As we stood in that otherworldly grove, the air heavy with the scent of earth and rebirth, I realized that perhaps the journey towards redemption was not one of solitude, but one shared with those who understood the pain of our pasts. And maybe, just maybe, forgiveness held the power to set us all free.

In the next few days, we arrived.

The air thinned as we ascended, the cold biting through our armor and right into our bones. Ahead, the Blackened Mountains loomed, a jagged and intimidating silhouette against the storm-laden sky. Majestic, yes, but filled with an overwhelming sense of foreboding that ran a shiver down my spine.

Every crevice and crag in the dark mountains was a shadowy maw, whispering the unknown dangers that lay ahead. The bleakness of the mountains was echoed in their moniker—Blackened.

"We stand on the cusp of destiny," I found myself murmuring, more to myself than to my companions.

Astrid, her auburn hair a vibrant contrast against the dreary backdrop, shifted her weight from one foot to another. Her green eyes were alight with an adventurous spark, reflecting the indomitable spirit that I'd come to admire. Her hand instinctively moved to the hilt of her sword, gripping it with an anticipation that echoed my own.

Thorkel, a figure of rugged solidity beside the restless Astrid, surveyed the mountain range with a grave quietude. His face was a weathered map of battles fought and tribulations overcome, his silent wisdom a comforting presence. A deep, knowing sigh escaped him as his gaze locked onto our path ahead, acknowledging the trials we were yet to face.

Erik, on the other hand, was a picture of silent strength. The familiar set of his jaw and the steadiness in his brown eyes reminded me so much of Siegfried that it was a painful balm.

Yet, there was a softness to him, a warmth that Siegfried never possessed. He offered me a reassuring smile, as if sensing my lingering ghosts.

"We have a mountain to conquer, my queen," Erik broke his silence, his voice as steadfast as his demeanor.

"Yes, we do," I replied, drawing a deep breath as I squared my shoulders and faced the Blackened Mountains, "and conquer we shall."

As I led my companions towards the daunting mountains, I could feel the echoes of our past merging with the pulse of our present. We were a motley group, each carrying our own burdens, yet unified in our purpose. Ahead lay a challenge that would test our mettle, but I had faith.

Faith in my comrades, faith in my redemption, and faith in the journey that awaited us in the shadowy heart of the Blackened Mountains.

13

The Ruthless Labyrinth

We stood there at the foot of the Blackened Mountain, our hearts filled with a mixture of anticipation and resolve. The mountain itself loomed over us, its towering presence both formidable and awe-inspiring. I could see the jagged silhouette of its dark peaks against the roiling, gray sky, the ominous clouds swirling like a tumultuous sea above. The distant howl of the wind was the only sound that dared break the profound silence, a chilling symphony that underscored our imminent trial.

With our eyes set on the battle that lay ahead, we had steeled ourselves for the inevitable confrontation with Fafnir or, at the very least, his formidable minions. Yet what we found at the entrance of a gaping cavern halfway up the slope was neither dragon nor beast, but an old man.

He was hunched, cloaked, and bore a worn face that told tales of a long, hard life. The old man was alone, the only sign of life amidst this desolate expanse of rock and wind.

"Welcome, weary travelers," he croaked, a slight grin playing on his weathered lips. His eyes sparkled with a hint of amusement that seemed oddly out of place, kindling a spark of suspicion in me.

"Who are you, old man?" I asked, my voice steady, echoing across the barren landscape. His presence was unexpected, his demeanor disconcerting. A sense of unease snaked its way around me, tightening its grip. Something felt off.

The old man's grin widened, his gaze flickering with an undecipherable emotion. "A simple guide, my dear," he replied, a cryptic undertone to his words.

His answer did little to quell my growing suspicion. A guide in this desolate wilderness? It seemed unlikely, yet the possibility that he might hold crucial knowledge about our impending battle with Fafnir spurred me to probe further.

"And why would we need a guide?" I questioned, crossing my arms over my chest. The wind whistled past us, kicking up a flurry of dust at our feet.

His gaze met mine, a spark of amusement dancing in his eyes. "Because, my dear Valkyrie," he paused, a knowing smile spreading across his face, "the true battle lies not ahead but within."

As the old man's words hung in the air, a shiver of realization ran through me. His cryptic message, the off-kilter amusement in his gaze—everything fell into place. We had been preparing for the wrong battle. With a last lingering look at the old man, we turned towards the gaping mouth of the cavern. As we stepped into the cave, the darkness swallowed us, and the old man's laughter echoed behind us, a haunting reminder of the twisted path that lay ahead.

A cool gust of wind swept past us, carrying an ethereal whisper of ancient secrets. My heart pounded in my chest as I led the group deeper into the cavernous hollow of the Blackened

Mountain. But as I ventured further, the uneven rocky walls around us started to shift, transitioning from craggy stone to smooth, labyrinthine passages that seemed to stretch infinitely in every direction.

With a gasp, I stopped in my tracks, looking around at the immense and twisting labyrinth that now surrounded us. Where the mountain cave had been, now stood tall walls of a maze, crafted from a material that bore a glossy sheen, as if the walls themselves were alive. The labyrinth seemed to breathe around us, the walls pulsating faintly with an ancient energy.

Astrid was the first to break the stunned silence. "By Odin's beard," she muttered, her fiery eyes wide as she studied the towering walls around us. "What sorcery is this?"

Thorkel, typically silent, grunted in acknowledgement of the inexplicable change. His usually unflappable demeanor was replaced with a furrowed brow and a tight grip on his weapon. Erik, on the other hand, remained quiet, his eyes darting around the maze with a mix of anxiety and curiosity.

My gaze turned inward, my mind whirling as I attempted to comprehend what had just happened. It wasn't a cave we'd entered, but a portal, one that had brought us here—into the Labyrinth of Jotnar. As the realization dawned, a chill ran down my spine, but I squared my shoulders, refusing to let my fear show.

"We move forward," I declared, looking each of my companions in the eyes. Their expressions echoed my determination; we were a group forged in the crucible of shared trials and tribulations. As we delved deeper into the labyrinth, I knew, without doubt, we were walking a path that would shape us in ways we could hardly imagine.

The further we ventured into the labyrinth, the less it felt like a simple structure of stone and magic. It became a mirror, reflecting back at us the very demons we'd tucked away in the deepest recesses of our hearts. Each twist and turn of the maze seemed to reach inside us, dredging up the buried fragments of our pasts.

The labyrinth knew my greatest regret—Siegfried. Every time I looked at Erik, I saw the ghost of my lost love. His gentle brown eyes, the contour of his face, the curve of his smile, all an eerie reminder of my past. The guilt welled up inside me, a poignant reminder of my transgressions. I was leading these brave souls, a fallen Valkyrie seeking redemption, towards an uncertain fate, just as I had led Siegfried to his end.

In the quiet moments, I caught Astrid staring into the distance, her usually fiery eyes clouded with an unknown sorrow. She had joined this journey with a spirit ablaze, eager to earn her place among the revered shieldmaidens. Yet, I knew her confidence was shaken, confronted by her doubts and the daunting task ahead. She would need to reconcile her ambition with the harsh reality of our journey.

Thorkel was an enigma, his stoic exterior hardly giving away any emotion. But I knew the labyrinth's magic was affecting him too. Late into the night, I saw him sitting alone, his hands tracing the faint scar on his cheek, a memento of a past battle. The labyrinth was making him face his own demons, ones he had locked away behind his rugged facade.

And then there was Erik, the young man burdened by a legacy he never asked for. His quiet strength, so akin to Siegfried's, was being tested as he too grappled with the labyrinth's trials. He was more than just a doppelganger of my lost love; he was a beacon of resilience and empathy that kept us grounded.

This was more than a physical journey through a maze. It

was a journey within, a confrontation with our pasts. It was the labyrinth's cruel yet necessary challenge, one that we had to overcome to find our redemption and the strength to face what lay ahead. As we navigated its winding corridors, we were also navigating the labyrinth within us, hoping to emerge stronger and more resolute.

The labyrinth was a harsh teacher, relentless and ruthless, testing us at every corner, pushing us to our limits. It wasn't just the sheer physicality of it, the icy stone beneath our feet, the endless winding paths stretching out into the gloom, but the deceptive illusions it spun around us.

A seemingly straight path would suddenly twist, leading us into treacherous terrain. A shadowy figure darted in the corners of our vision, causing alarm and anticipation. Illusions of dread-inducing monsters lurked behind corners, turning our hearts to ice only to dissipate into smoke upon confrontation.

Yet, it was in the crucible of these challenges that we found our strength. Our unity was our lifeline. We learned to trust each other's instincts, depend on each other's strengths. We discovered Astrid's uncanny ability to read the deceptive illusions, the keen wisdom hidden behind Thorkel's rugged exterior, Erik's quiet resilience guiding us when our spirits flagged.

The labyrinth forced us to grapple with fear and doubt, to face the stark reality of our journey. It was a cruel reminder of the path we'd chosen, fraught with danger and uncertainty. But in its twisted, merciless way, it was also forging us into a team, honing our spirits for the battle ahead.

Through every test and trial, the calling of our quest resounded within each of us. It echoed off the labyrinth's stone walls, flowed in our blood, and nestled in our hearts. It was a constant reminder, a beacon in the eerie gloom, a rallying cry against despair.

Our determination hardened. Each challenge, each test, each deceptive turn of the labyrinth only served to solidify our resolve. We were more than just four lost souls thrown together by fate. We were a team, a band of warriors bound by a shared purpose.

As we navigated the labyrinth, our bond deepened. We faced the labyrinth not as individuals but as a united front, ready to brave any storm, fight any foe, confront any demon. The labyrinth was testing us, but in its ruthless trials, it was also forging us into something greater. It was our crucible, and we would emerge stronger, prepared for whatever lay ahead.

14

The Echoes of Forgiveness

The labyrinth was teeming with mythical creatures, each encounter turning the pages of ancient tales and the stuff of legends into our stark reality. Their presence was a manifestation of the labyrinth's inherent magic, a hint of the world's essence we were intruding upon.

We met a Nixie by a subterranean river, her form shifting and shimmering with every movement. She was as capricious as the water she commanded, her gaze both gentle and fierce. With a riddle as elusive as her nature, she pointed us towards a less treacherous path.

The Svartalfar, dark elves known for their cunning and craft, lurked in the deeper recesses. Their eyes gleamed like precious gems in the dark, their fingers weaving illusions that threatened to throw us off our path. Yet, we learned to see through their deception, the sharp wit of Astrid coming to our rescue more than once.

Then there was the Jötnar, an ice giant trapped within the heart of the labyrinth. With a sorrowful countenance that mirrored the icicles dangling from his beard, he challenged us to a battle of might. Despite his towering size, he moved with a grace that belied his stature. It was Thorkel's seasoned experience and Erik's unyielding determination that eventually won us the bout and a crucial clue to our quest.

Each encounter was a test of our strength, wits, and unity. Yet, with each test, we were evolving, our bonds deepening. We started to anticipate each other's moves, cover each other's weaknesses. We celebrated our victories together and shared our defeats. We laughed and cried, fought and reconciled. We shared the weight of our journey, our goals, our fears.

In this labyrinth of the gods, amidst trials and mythical beings, we found each other. We became more than just a group thrown together by fate; we became companions, comrades, friends. We learned to rely on each other, trust each other, and more importantly, understand each other.

Every creature, every encounter, every shared moment was shaping us, guiding us, pushing us towards our destiny. In the mystical heart of the labyrinth, under the watchful eyes of ancient beings, we were becoming more than what we were.

The labyrinth seemed to peer into our souls, unearthing the ghosts of our past and painting them on its ancient walls. We walked through a series of chambers, each one a mirror of our past, a riddle spun from our own mistakes and regrets.

For me, the vision was that of Siegfried, the noble warrior I had loved, now fallen by my own hands. The echo of his last breath, the life fading from his eyes, the chill of his lifeless body — it was all too real. The walls of the labyrinth echoed with my guilt and shame, resounding with my silent screams of regret. Yet, amidst the torment, I found a hint of redemption. I chose to face my guilt, to hold it, accept it, learn from it. And with that acceptance, I found a small measure of peace.

Astrid faced her own reflections. I watched her wrestle with the vision of herself draped in royal regalia, her eyes gleaming with unfulfilled ambitions, her hands bloodied by the sacrifices she had made. Her struggle was intense, a battle against herself. But in the end, she emerged victorious, her fiery spirit kindled, her resolve hardened. The labyrinth had tested her ambition, and she had reforged it into a purpose.

Thorkel's past was a mural of battles, each victory etched with the blood of his enemies, each defeat a scar on his soul. The labyrinth mocked him with the faces of those he had slain, the cries of those he had failed. But Thorkel, our stoic warrior, stood tall. He bore his sins and bore them well. He did not shy away from his past but confronted it, his remorse a sign of his humanity. The labyrinth had unveiled his sins, and he had found the courage to atone.

Erik's trial was one of silence. His was a mirror filled with hushed whispers, unvoiced desires, and stifled cries. His insecurities loomed like shadows, lashing out, seeking to engulf him. But Erik fought. His quiet resolve, his silent strength became his shield. He stood up to his insecurities, his voice breaking the silence, shattering his fears. The labyrinth had whispered his doubts, and he had answered with courage.

The labyrinth pushed us, tested us, tormented us. It drew out our fears and laid our sins bare. But we stood strong. We faced our past, wrestled with our demons, and emerged stronger. We took our fears, our regrets, our guilt and turned them into our strength. We pushed forward, our determination fueling us.

For me, the labyrinth was not just a maze of stone and magic—it was a mirror. Every turn, every corner, every echoing footstep was a ghost of my past, each whispering a memory, each howling a mistake. My transgressions seemed magnified here, refracting through the labyrinth's heart like malevolent spectres. I felt their weight, like a shroud, thick and heavy, threatening to drag me under.

Each challenge of the labyrinth, each riddle, seemed tailor-made to prey on my guilt. The stone mocked me, hissed at me, each test a cruel reminder of my past. It gnawed at my resolve, peeled away at my determination layer by layer, but I continued. I had no choice but to keep moving, for the spectre of failure was far worse than the spectre of regret.

Through the oppressive weight of my remorse, there was a flicker of something else—resonance. It emanated from the ancient artifact in my hand, the Gungnir's Echo. It was a rhythmic hum, a palpable energy that harmonized with the beat of my heart, the thrum of my soul. It was unnerving at first, this connection—so deep, so personal. It felt like an intrusion, a violation, but there was no denying the raw power it brought.

At first, this power felt chaotic, uncontrollable. It burned, it stung, it rattled my very core. The labyrinth shook under its influence, its walls shivering as if in fear. It was too much, too intense. But, in the heart of this chaos, I found a strange sense of clarity.

The labyrinth, for all its torment, was a teacher. Through its trials, I came face to face with my past and realized the undeniable truth—I was the cause of my own suffering. My guilt, my regret, they were chains I had forged myself, shackles of my own design.

Once I understood this, once I accepted my mistakes, not as an inexorable sentence but as lessons learned, the Echo responded. The searing chaos eased into a warm embrace, a resonant hum of understanding. The Echo, in its arcane wisdom, didn't chastise me for my past but celebrated my acceptance of it. It grew stronger, bolder, the pulses of power echoing my newfound resolve.

Through my trials in this haunting labyrinth, I had found something precious—forgiveness. A concept so simple yet so intricate, like a web spun of gossamer threads, beautiful yet easily torn apart by the weight of guilt. It whispered around me, entwining with the echoes of Gungnir in my grip, pulsing like a heartbeat. I grappled with it, wrestling against years of self-condemnation and regret. The labyrinth watched, silent, expectant.

The Echo guided me, a mentor in this strange dance with forgiveness. It showed me a past painted not in hues of guilt, but of learning. A past where every mistake was a stepping stone, every regret a lesson, every moment an opportunity. I saw myself, not as the fallen queen, but as a woman who dared to love, dared to dream, and dared to fail. The Echo taught me, whispering, "You can't change what was, but you can accept what is."

As I embrace this new truth, I felt a transformation. It began like a small ember, kindled deep within me, warming me, healing me. It spread, not like a wildfire, but like a gentle sunrise, quietly chasing away the darkness of self-doubt and guilt. I stood taller, my spine no longer bowed under the weight of regret.

My companions—Astrid, Thorkel, Erik—began to see this change. The heaviness in our conversations fades, replaced by a newfound confidence in my words. My decisions, once cautious and tentative, were now assertive and decisive. I saw them respond to this shift, their eyes reflecting a mix of surprise and admiration.

And Gungnir's Echo? It no longer felt like a burden, a tormentor. It felt... right. It pulsed in time with my heartbeat, a symphony of acceptance and forgiveness. It responded to my touch, to my intent, transforming from an enigmatic relic into a powerful tool.

My newfound strength and mastery over the Echo were put to the test when we encountered a mythical beast within the labyrinth. A leviathan, wreathed in shadow and menace, blocked our path. But I was no longer the queen who trembled at her past. I was Brunhilde, the warrior, guided by Gungnir's Echo, fueled by forgiveness. My victory over the beast wasn't just a physical triumph—it was a testament to my spiritual transformation.

As the beast fell, I stood amongst my companions, my heart pounding, not with fear, but triumph. I looked around, my gaze meeting the proud eyes of Astrid, the warm smile of Erik, the respectful nod of Thorkel. I realized then, I was not just on a path to redemption. I was living it. I was reborn within the heart of the labyrinth, no longer bound by the chains of my past but freed by the echoes of forgiveness.

15

The Master of Deception

There was a certain hush that fell upon us as we reached the labyrinth's core. The chaotic twists and turns gave way to a cavernous hall, a grand finale staged within the heart of the icy fortress. It was the calm before the storm, the quiet before the chaos. And then it arrived—the storm, the chaos, the nemesis of our journey.

Emerging from the shadows, it coiled within the room—a creature so colossal, so terrifying, that it turned the air frigid. The ice serpent. Its scales glistened like frozen teardrops, eyes twin sapphires that burned with a chilling glint. It was beautiful in a deadly way, a predator in its prime, exuding an aura of impending doom. A chill, more profound than any winter's touch, crawled up our spines.

We knew what this means. There was no other path, no other choice. It was us or the serpent.

Erik, ever silent, ever watchful, stepped forward. There was a striking familiarity in his stance, a shadow of a memory. Siegfried. My heart clenched. The echoes of the past entwined with the thrumming present, the lines blurring, the specter of fear rising. Not again. I could not lose him too.

Our weapons clashed against the beast's scales, a symphony of survival resounding within the labyrinth's heart. Erik moved with a grace that belies the seriousness of our situation, his maneuvers reminiscent of a dance. But the serpent was quick, relentless. In the blur of the confrontation, a piercing cry rent the air. Erik crumpled to the ground, a scarlet stain blossoming against the snow.

Memories rushed in—a flash of silver, a gasp of pain, a life slipping through my fingers. Siegfried. The echo of my grief, my guilt, reverberated through the labyrinth, drowning me in a sea of despair. Erik, so much like Siegfried, lay on the frosty floor, the pallor of his face a ghostly contrast to the pooling red. The fear, the pain, the helplessness—all returned with a vengeance. I was on the precipice again, the fear of loss clawing at my soul.

But this was not the past. And I was not the same. The labyrinth had changed me, and so had Erik. His soft smiles, his silent support, his unwavering belief in me—flashed through my mind. I refused to let the past repeat itself. I refused to lose Erik.

Gungnir's Echo pulsed, syncing with my heartbeat, my resolve. The labyrinth's trials, my trials, had prepared me for this moment. Forged in the fires of guilt and bathed in the soothing balm of forgiveness, I stood, my determination etched in every line of my body.

This was our battle. Our path to redemption. We would not falter. We would not fall. The serpent would not win.

With a resonating roar, I launched myself at the beast. Every clash, every thrust, every dodge—it was a dance, a narrative of my journey painted in the language of battle. It was my guilt, my redemption, my acceptance, mirrored in the icy serpent's eyes. This was not just a fight for survival—it was a symbolic death, a shedding of my old self, and a birth of the new.

Each blow was a testament to my courage, each scar a badge of my resolve. I fought with an intensity that blazed brighter than Astrid's spirit, every strike echoed Thorkel's wisdom, and each defense mirrored Erik's silent support. It was not a solitary battle—it was a symphony of our shared journey, our shared trials, our shared redemption.

In the heart of the labyrinth, I struck the final blow. The ice serpent shrieked, its death cry resonating with the echoes of Gungnir. As it slumped, its life extinguished, a sense of tranquility settled over the labyrinth—a silent acknowledgement of our victory.

There I stood, amidst the stillness, draped in the echoes of my past and present, my heart brimming with newfound strength. I was not the queen who had failed her king—I was the shieldmaiden who had overcome her past. The slaying of the serpent was not just the end of a creature—it was a symbol, a testament to my growth, a proclamation of my redemption.

In the chilling aftermath of the battle, the serpent's defeat echoed through the labyrinth, its last wailing cry reverberating off the cold stone walls. As the creature's massive form began to disintegrate into a cascade of icy shards, my attention turned towards Erik. He lay wounded on the ground, the intensity of the fight etched on his pallid face.

We had won this battle, but our war was far from over. The labyrinth had tested us, strengthened our resolve, and deepened our bonds. Our victory over the serpent was but a stepping stone on a journey that still stretched far ahead, filled with shared trials and the promise of redemption.

Before I could tend to Erik, a sudden tremor seized the

labyrinth, and the icy walls around us began to shift and blur. It felt as if the very fabric of reality was being torn apart, replaced by something utterly alien. A dizzying whirlwind of sensations engulfed us. It felt as though we were being drawn inwards, spiraling down into an unseen vortex.

As the sensation subsided, we found ourselves standing in a place unlike any we had seen before. It was a grand hall, gilded and glorious, with high vaulted ceilings and walls adorned with intricate, shimmering runes. Dominating the hall was an imposing throne, carved from what appeared to be a massive, gnarled tree, its branches twisted and turned into elegant loops and arches.

Sitting on the throne was the old man we had met at the mouth of the cave. But he was changed. His form shimmered and shifted as if caught in a haze. Suddenly, his aged exterior peeled away, revealing a figure of majestic stature. He was clad in green and gold, his hair fiery red and eyes gleaming with an intelligence that was sharp and disconcerting. The frail old man had been nothing more than a facade. Here, in all his resplendent glory, was Loki, the trickster god himself.

His eyes met mine, and he smiled, a mischievous smirk that betrayed hidden motives yet to be deciphered. "So we meet again, Brunhilde," he said, his voice resonating throughout the hall. The transformation was striking, and his true identity was as alarming as it was unexpected. "I see you've survived the Labyrinth of Jotnar."

Survived, but not unscathed. There we stood before him, battered and bruised yet unyielding in our determination. We had braved his labyrinth, faced its trials, and emerged stronger. We were ready for whatever else he might throw at us. Loki, the master of deception, had become our new challenge, and we would face him, head on.

"Your labyrinth was but a detour," I retorted, my gaze unyielding. "Our quest continues."

"Oh, indeed it does," Loki replied, his grin broadening. His eyes flicked to Erik, lying unconscious in Astrid's arms. "Though it seems you've sustained some losses."

His words hung in the air like a threat, a premonition of trials yet to come.

16

The Towering World Tree

A surge of anger welled up inside me as I stood before Loki. This god had spun a web of deception, manipulating us like puppets in his grand scheme. His gaze was cool, composed, but beneath that composed exterior, I sensed a keen anticipation, like a cat toying with its prey.

"Is this your idea of a jest, Loki?" I demanded, my voice echoing throughout the grand hall. "Playing with our lives to stop us from defeating Fafnir?"

His response was a rich, mirthful laugh that reverberated around us. "Oh, Brunhilde, is that what you think?" he asked, a glint of amusement in his sharp eyes. His mockery stung, fueling my ire. But before I could retort, he started to explain.

"My dear, your journey into the labyrinth was not designed to thwart you," he began, leaning back casually in his imposing throne. His gaze swept over us, taking in our ragged forms, our wary expressions. "No, it was a test, a crucible designed to prepare you for the battle against Fafnir."

He let his words sink in, the weight of his revelation casting a blanket of stunned silence over us. My mind raced, grappling with the implications of his statement. Could it be possible? Was Loki not our foe, but a perverse guide in our quest?

"I was the one who called you from your isolation in the Isle of Forgotten Heroes, Brunhilde," he continued, his gaze fixing on me again. His words echoed in my mind, adding to my swirling confusion.

Betrayal, relief, and confusion mingled within me, battling for dominance. I felt the eyes of my companions on me, each of them grappling with their own emotions. The silence of the hall was broken only by Loki's chuckling.

The god's revelation created a storm of thoughts in our minds. Anger for his deceptive methods, relief that we had not been thrown off our mission, and confusion over his role in our journey. Our quest had been twisted and turned by the whims of the Trickster, and all we could do was try to make sense of it all. In this grand game of gods and mortals, it seemed we were but pawns, and Loki, the player making his unpredictable moves.

"Why you, Loki?" I asked, my voice echoing through the grand hall. "Why not Odin, or any of the other gods who have tasked me with facing Fafnir? And why should we believe a word you say?"

My questions were met with a cacophony of laughter from Loki, who appeared to be immensely amused by my bold confrontation.

"Ah, Brunhilde, ever the warrior, ever the skeptic," he chuckled, resting his chin on his intertwined fingers. "Isn't it intriguing? The why's and the how's, the intricate web of fate and destiny?"

His emerald eyes twinkled mischievously as he leaned forward, the weight of his words settling like a cloak around us. His next words were spoken with an air of irreverence that only a god could afford.

"You know, it doesn't really matter whether you believe me or not," he said, his voice echoing in the high arches of the hall. "What truly matters is what you feel, what you've become through this ordeal." His words, as cryptic as they were, held a strange sense of truth.

The hall fell silent, his last statement resonating within us. Loki, the trickster god, had guided our journey and our growth without us knowing. Despite the resentment we felt, we could not ignore the growth we had experienced in the labyrinth.

We had delved into our fears, faced our past, and emerged stronger. We had forged bonds, battled monsters, and learned more about ourselves than we ever thought possible. It was an undeniable truth—our journey in the labyrinth had been crucial to our development.

As I looked at my companions, their faces thoughtful, their eyes resolute, I felt a sense of solidarity. We were united, stronger, and better equipped for the trials that awaited us. The daunting task of facing Fafnir seemed less terrifying now. Loki's revelations had sparked a fire within us—a fire of determination and resolve.

Each of us processed Loki's words in our own way, but we all understood that we had emerged from the labyrinth not as victims of Loki's trickery, but as warriors ready to face our destiny.

"I still don't understand why you did this, Loki," I confessed, my voice echoing through the cavernous hall. "But, I suppose in a strange way, you've guided me towards a path of redemption. And for that, I thank you." I held his gaze, meeting the flicker of surprise that danced in his emerald eyes. "And after this, what should we do?"

A chuckle escaped Loki, his eyes sparkling with a mischievous glint. "You're welcome, Brunhilde," he replied with a theatrical bow. "But as for your next step... well, you'll find the answer on your way out. See you later, my dear children."

Leaving behind the grandeur of the hall and the riddling god, we emerged into the open air. The echo of Loki's laughter, eerie yet strangely comforting, lingered behind us. As we stepped into the new environment, a gasp caught in my throat. We stood at the mouth of an expansive valley, its beauty so raw and untamed it was breathtaking.

Verdant meadows unfurled before us, stretching to the edge of the horizon, painted in the vibrant hues of the wildflowers dotting the landscape. A river, gleaming under the midday sun, snaked its way through the valley, the gentle rush of its waters a soft whisper in the breeze. High cliffs, their faces scarred by the passage of time, flanked the valley, standing as silent guardians over the serene landscape.

But it was the sight far in the distance that truly took our breath away. Rising from the heart of the valley was Yggdrasil, the World Tree. Its grandeur was indescribable, its canopy reaching out to the heavens, its roots disappearing into the depths of the earth. A shroud of mist wrapped around its trunk, lending an ethereal air to its majestic form. It stood as a beacon, its presence resonating with an ageless wisdom that seemed to call out to us.

The sight of Yggdrasil stirred a deep-seated emotion within us. It was not just the physical embodiment of the interconnectedness of the nine realms, but also a symbol of our journey. Our path was intertwined, knotted, and rooted deep, much like the branches of the World Tree. We had traversed through our past, delved into our fears, and now, we were ready to reach out to our future, to face Fafnir.

As we set forth towards the towering Yggdrasil, the valley echoing with the call of the wild, I felt a sense of purpose. Loki's riddles and the labyrinth's trials had prepared us for this. We were ready, we were strong, and we were united. The World Tree awaited us, and so did our destiny.

17

The Quiet Moments

The chill of Loki's grand hall still clung to us as we took our first steps outside, away from the veiled throne and towards the vast expanse of the valley that lay before us. I could feel the weight of Gungnir's Echo hanging lightly at my side, a constant reminder of the lessons learned and the strength discovered within myself. No longer was I the guilt-ridden shade of the warrior I once was. Through trials and tribulation, I had begun to reconcile with my past, forging a path towards redemption.

My gaze locked onto the distant peak of Yggdrasil, our next destination. Its summit piercing the celestial canvas was a silent sentinel among the swirling nebulae of the Northern Lights. It was a breathtaking vista—a majestic testament to the awe-inspiring landscapes of our mythological world.

The air around us was crisp, each breath a stark reminder of our shifting environment. Astrid walked beside me, her gaze firmly set on the path ahead. She was different, too. The raw ambition that had initially defined her had transformed into a tempered resolve. She had learnt to value the journey as much as the destination, her understanding of power and leadership expanded through the trials we'd faced together.

As for Thorkel, the daunting valley before us was but another chapter in his journey towards redemption. He was no longer the proud, fiery warrior I'd first met. He'd faced his past sins in the labyrinth, emerging humbled and reflective. I saw a tranquility in him now, a peace born out of acceptance and resolution.

Beside Thorkel, Erik's transformation was perhaps the most surprising. Despite his youthful exterior, he carried the strength and resilience of someone who had been through the wringer of self-doubt and emerged stronger on the other side. The boy who had entered the labyrinth filled with insecurities was now a young man of resolve and bravery, his eyes holding a spark that was hard to ignore.

As we traversed the diverse terrains, from barren, frost-kissed plains to treacherous, shadowy forests, we found our rhythm as a team. The labyrinth had served to peel back our layers, revealing the raw, unvarnished truths of our characters. The shared struggle deepened our understanding of each other. Each step closer to Yggdrasil was another step in our shared journey—laden with tales and laughter.

I remember one night, as we sat around our campfire, Thorkel broke the silence. "Remember the time in the labyrinth when I almost fell into the abyss, only to be saved by a talking raven?" He shook his head, his grin catching the firelight, "Who would've thought that a bird would have more wisdom than a seasoned warrior?"

Astrid let out a bark of laughter. "Well, Thorkel, perhaps if you used your ears as much as your fists, you wouldn't need birds to save you." Thorkel looked mock-offended, and the laughter that rang through our camp was a balm to our weary hearts.

Then, Erik, always curious, asked me, "Brunhilde, when you were a shieldmaiden, what was the most challenging opponent you faced?"

I took a moment to remember, then answered, "A fearsome frost giant who had almost the same stubbornness as Astrid."

Astrid simply smirked at my light-hearted jab, clearly enjoying the banter.

These moments of laughter, shared tales, and light-hearted jabs breathed life into our strenuous journey. They made the burden of the journey seem lighter, the nights less cold, the road less lonely.

But amidst the camaraderie, there was also room for earnest conversations. One night, under a blanket of countless stars, Astrid turned to me, her eyes reflecting the twinkling constellations, "Brunhilde," she began, her voice a whisper against the night, "how did you learn to...forgive yourself?"

The question, simple yet laden with depth, hung in the cold air between us. A mirror to my soul, it echoed the tumultuous journey of self-discovery that had led me here. I felt a smile tugging at the corners of my lips, a bitter-sweet mix of the pain of the past and the hope for the future.

"I'm still learning, Astrid," I confessed, my voice barely louder than the rustling leaves around us. I took a deep breath, the cool night air filling my lungs. "It's not a destination, but a journey. A journey of understanding and accepting that we're all flawed. That mistakes are not failures, but opportunities to grow."

Her eyes softened, a veil lifting as if she was seeing me, truly seeing me, for the first time. And that opened the floodgates. In the cloak of the dark, under the silent witness of the stars, we poured out our hearts. Thorkel spoke of his lost homeland, his words painting a vivid picture of green valleys, roaring rivers, and towering mountains. The home he missed so dearly became real in our minds, its beauty bittersweet in its absence. Afterward, Erik confessed his fear of not living up to the legacy of his forebears, his words a poignant testament to the burdens we carry.

We spoke not as warriors on a quest, but as human beings, each carrying our own burden of guilt and regret. We listened and understood, offering solace and empathy. We saw each other's scars and the strength it took to bear them.

The labyrinth had bound us together, but it was these quiet moments, these shared stories, and shared vulnerabilities that turned us into more than just companions. They reminded us that despite our individual battles, we were never alone. This time of peace served as a quiet cocoon, fostering a deepening bond among us.

Then, the ceaseless stride of our journey finally ebbed as the silhouette of Yggdrasil, the World Tree, rose from the horizon. A sense of awe permeated the air, the sight of the mighty tree and its branches spreading wide towards the heavens stirred something within us, a stirring akin to reverence.

The trunk, gnarled with wisdom beyond time, stretched upwards, its extremities seeming to tickle the belly of the sky. Its roots, veiny and entrenched, delved deep into the core of the earth, a poetic mirroring of how the past shaped the present and future. In the presence of this silent giant, we were but mere specks. Yet, the onus of protecting this behemoth, the very heartbeat of our existence, had fallen onto our weary shoulders. The magnitude of our mission sat heavy on us, the silent reminder of what was at stake – our world.

As we stood under the leafy canopies, bathing in the last light of the setting sun, we took a moment to look back at the twisting path that led us here. The trials of the labyrinth seemed a lifetime away, the fears, the battles, the loss, and the victories – they had carved us, honed us into the warriors we were now. We had grown, not just in strength, but in understanding – understanding of ourselves and each other.

We found solace in the unity we had fostered during our quest. The friendships we had formed stood as our bedrock, an unyielding fortress against the fear and doubt that threatened to seep in. As we huddled together, we made a pact under the sprawling boughs of Yggdrasil, to stand united against whatever lay ahead. The shadows of the night grew long, swallowing the last vestiges of the day, but our determination held steadfast, our resolve unbroken.

The stillness of the night was a stark contrast to the raging storm of anticipation within us. An invisible clock ticked away, each second bringing us closer to our confrontation with Fafnir. Yet, there was calm amidst the brewing tempest. We found peace in the pregnant pause before the inevitable battle. As we rested under the watchful presence of Yggdrasil, hearts brimming with the weight of our destiny, we were ready. Ready to face the final chapter of our saga.

18

The Shadow of Destruction

The chill swept over me, not born of the cold wind, but from the dread seeping into my bones as we neared the heart of Yggdrasil. The sky overhead darkened, not with the cloak of nightfall, but with the massive, sprawling form of Fafnir. The once vibrant tapestry of the forest was now a somber canvas of dread, each leaf and twig trembling under the monstrous shadow of our adversary.

He was the embodiment of our deepest fears, his form an unfathomable nightmare against the backdrop of the great World Tree. His monstrous silhouette stretched across the horizon, a terrifying testament to the destructive power he possessed. Each heavy beat of his wings was a thunderous declaration of his might, resonating within the very core of Yggdrasil, and within us.

His cruel eyes, orbs of liquid fire, burned through the murk, locking onto us with a terrifying acuity. His sulfurous breath curled in the frosty air, an insidious poison spreading through the once pristine grove. The sight of him brought reality crashing down around us; Fafnir wasn't just a legend or a story told to frighten children, he was real, he was here, and he stood between us and the preservation of our world.

The tension seemed to hum in the air, a vibration that thrummed against our skin, curled around our bones, charging the atmosphere with an ominous energy. The rhythmic thudding of our hearts matched the cadence of an echoing drumbeat – the heartbeat of Fafnir. Each resonant pulse a stark reminder of the colossal beast we stood against, the creature whose insatiable greed dared to encroach upon Yggdrasil, the World Tree, the heart of existence itself.

Thorkel broke the silence, his voice ringing hollow against the vast expanse surrounding us. "I suppose there's no negotiating with him, is there?" His attempt at humor was but a thinly veiled mask, barely disguising the tension that strained his words.

I cast a sidelong glance at him, my grip tightening around the smooth, cold shaft of Gungnir's Echo, the weapon that held a fragment of Odin's own might. "I'm afraid not," I replied, the words slipping past my lips cloaked in grim resolve. For this was not a beast that understood reason or mercy, this was a creature twisted by avarice and hunger for power, a dragon born from a Dwarf's greed and a cursed gold's wrath.

I could feel the flutter of fear, the shadow of doubt that threatened to cloud my mind. Could we truly succeed against such a formidable adversary? Could we protect our world from the monstrous specter of destruction looming over us, as grand and terrifying as the darkness itself?

I quashed those doubts, pushed them away to the far recesses of my mind. This was not the time for fear, not when we stood at the precipice of our destiny. This was the time for courage, for unity, for the unwavering belief that we could, and we would, safeguard our world. For as long as breath filled our lungs and courage ignited our spirits, we would not let Fafnir claim Yggdrasil, no matter the cost.

With a shared nod of understanding, we tightened our ranks, steeling ourselves for the inevitable clash. The dark shape of Fafnir seemed to swell, looming even larger as we approached. We walked towards the beast, towards the battle that awaited us, our spirits burning brighter against the shadow of despair. This was our time. Our test.

With a look exchanged between us, silent words passed and understood, we charged forward, launching ourselves into the heart of battle.

Erik, the young warrior whose bravery outmatched his years, struck with precision, his ax splitting the air with a ferocity that mirrored his determined spirit. Thorkel, the giant of a man whose humor hid a depth of wisdom, wielded his hammer with an unwavering strength, a testament to his relentless spirit. Astrid, the maiden of the bow, her every arrow finding its mark, proved that grace and ferocity could indeed coexist.

My spear danced with deadly grace, every thrust and parry a word in the poem of our battle, every heartbeat a drumbeat spurring us forward. The energy around us was electric, a pulsing, living entity born of our shared determination and will. Each of us, in our own way, contributed to the symphony of battle.

We moved as one, our individual strengths and skills merging into a single, formidable force. We were warriors from different paths, bound by a shared destiny and a common enemy. In this moment, amidst the chaos and the clamor, our unity was our most powerful weapon against Fafnir's monstrous form.

The heat of battle clung to us like a second skin, but my golden spear glistened in my right hand, a physical manifestation of my resolve, while Gungnir's Echo, the embodiment of Odin's might, hummed with latent power in my left.

I stood at the forefront, an unyielding bulwark against Fafnir's relentless onslaught. Every sweep of his monstrous tail, every gout of his searing flame, met the unwavering defense of Gungnir's Echo. With every parry and dodge, I could feel my command over the legendary staff growing, as if the weapon itself acknowledged my worthiness.

It was more than just a fight. It was a dance, a ballet of flashes and clangs, of deadly grace and raw power. And at the heart of it all was me, a true Valkyrie, no longer fallen but rising.

The battlefield raged like a furious storm, Fafnir's assault pressing us relentlessly, each devastating blow like a hammer against our resolve. His monstrous form seemed to embody the very essence of destruction, the ground shaking beneath his every step, and his roar reverberating through the air, as if challenging the very heavens themselves.

Fafnir's wrath seemed insurmountable. His flames danced around us like vengeful spirits, searing the air, the heat a living entity that sought to consume us. His tail lashed out like a lightning strike, fierce and sudden, and his claws cut through the air with deadly precision.

Yet, our resolve did not falter. Each blow we took only hardened our determination, for we knew the stakes. We were not just fighting for ourselves, but for every soul that breathed under the sky, for every tree that swayed in the wind, for every ripple that danced upon the seas.

Our unity was our bulwark against the storm of destruction. We rallied around each other, a fortress of flesh and bone against the onslaught. Thorkel, our immovable stone, met the dragon's fury with his own. Astrid's arrows cut through the haze of battle, each a silver streak of defiance. Erik stood at my side, his axes singing their own song of resistance.

I found a strength within me. My arms ached from wielding the twin weights of my golden spear and Gungnir's Echo, yet I held them aloft, a bastion against the chaos. We fought as one, our individual strengths woven into a tapestry of resilience. Our bodies may have bled, our breaths may have labored, but our spirits remained unbroken. Beneath the shadow of destruction, our determination shone bright.

With a bellow that echoed across the yawning expanse of the World Tree's heart, Fafnir lunged. It was his ultimate attack. His monstrous form was a terrifying spectacle, a grotesque manifestation of destruction and chaos. Thorkel stepped forward, his hardened eyes gleaming with a fierce resolve. In his hand was his hammer, worn and chipped, a testament to a lifetime of battles, of victories, and defeats. He met the beast's assault head-on, his sacrifice allowing us the precious seconds we needed.

As a primal roar tore its way from my throat, I charged. It was the time. Now or never. My golden spear became an extension of myself, piercing the air as I hurtled towards the cursed dragon that was Fafnir. Behind me, a torrent of power erupted, the collective might of my companions forging a palpable, pulsating force. It was strength, hope, faith, all interwoven and surging into me, filling every sinew, every cell.

I drank deeply of this potent energy, channeling it through the very marrow of my bones, guiding it towards the waiting vessel that was Gungnir's Echo. The legendary weapon in my left hand seemed to awaken in response, humming with an alien vibrancy, its form limned with an ethereal, otherworldly luminescence.

Harnessing every ounce of our shared might, every sliver of our combined resolve, I struck. Gungnir's Echo sliced through the air, lancing into the heart of the monstrous beast before us. Its ethereal light seared through Fafnir's shadowy form, a radiant beacon against the pulsating darkness. The behemoth responded with a roar, a thunderous bellow that seemed to shake the very heart of Yggdrasil.

The ground beneath us heaved, quaking in time with Fafnir's final, shuddering collapse. The terrible titan lay vanquished, his reign of terror extinguished by the unwavering resolve of those who dared to challenge him.

Astrid, Erik, and I stood trembling, gasping for breath amidst the settling dust. Then, we turned, a chilling realization descending upon us like a funeral shroud. Thorkel, our trusted comrade, lay still, a stone's throw from Fafnir's still-twitching corpse.

His silent form was a painful testament to the high cost of our victory. The seasoned warrior, whose mettle had been forged in the crucible of countless battles, had given his last full measure of devotion to a cause greater than his own existence.

We gathered around Thorkel, our hearts heavy with grief. This hardened veteran had found his redemption not in words, but through his actions, his indomitable courage in the face of seemingly insurmountable odds. His final act of sacrifice echoed louder than any battle cry.

"Erik," I said, my voice barely above a whisper, my eyes never leaving Thorkel. "Share his tale. Ensure it is remembered."

Erik nodded, his eyes shining with unshed tears. "Aye. He earned that much."

19

The Tale of Victory

The battlefield stood silent now. Amidst the remnants of Fafnir, the embers of our victory flickered, casting long, somber shadows. Through the settling dust, I saw the remnants of our battle, scattered haphazardly around the field like a perverse tribute to the monstrosity we had vanquished. Burnt patches of earth, scorched by dragonfire, painted a grim picture, while the shadows of destruction leered at us from every corner.

Victory, they call it. It was a great victory. But it was also a word that tasted bitter on my tongue, poisoned by the void Thorkel left behind. A hollow triumph, akin to the fallen leaves that flutter down from Yggdrasil. Each leaf, a tale of glory, ended up as nothing more than a whisper in the wind, forgotten and abandoned, much like our joy in the aftermath of Fafnir's defeat.

As the wind picked up, it carried with it the scent of smoldering earth and charred flesh. It howled our victory to the heavens, a melancholic melody that permeated the stillness around us. Yet, as the triumphant notes reached my ears, they morphed into a solemn dirge. My heart picked up the rhythm, each beat pounding out Thorkel's name like a grim mantra echoing through the hollowness.

Astrid stood beside me, bathed in the gloaming light. Her auburn hair, usually as vibrant as a phoenix's plume, appeared dim under the sorrowful sky, each strand a testament to our shared grief. Her emerald eyes, windows to her fiery spirit, now reflected my own torment, mirroring the deep-seated pain I feel.

Erik, his sandy blond hair rustling in the breeze, stood as the quiet counterpoint to our quiet grief. He had always been our anchor, the peace amidst our storm. But now, his usually bright brown eyes were dimmed, his gaze fixed on the vacant space where Thorkel would have stood. In the end, we were but wayfarers, set on our individual paths, bound by our collective loss.

I stood at the base of Yggdrasil, its vibrant energy pulsating against my palm, a heartbeat shared across the realms. It was a connection I had always cherished, a reminder of the intricate web of life that ties us all together. The roots of Yggdrasil, eternally nurturing, drew up the ancient energy from the ground, feeding life into the endless cosmos above.

With a silent prayer to the departed warrior, I laid my hand on the gnarled bark. I whispered words of old, the ancient tongue rolling off my tongue as I invoked the tree's power, asking for safe passage. A spark of magic danced along my skin, a warm sensation that seeped into the tree, spreading through its roots and branches. The air thickened around us, and a sense of profound calm blanketed the battlefield, a stark contrast to the violent confrontation we had just survived.

A luminous pathway opened, a portal into the roots of Yggdrasil. We stepped through, leaving behind the battlefield, and the spectral echo of Fafnir's presence. It was a strange sensation, as if we were adrift in a cosmic ocean, currents of raw energy carrying us away. Yggdrasil cradled us, guiding us through its immense network, its branches stretching out like veins throughout the realms.

As the blinding light recedes, we found ourselves at the foot of a mountain range, its towering peaks dusted with snow. The chill air cut through our weariness, a sharp reminder of our reality. Yggdrasil had transported us near the Blackened Mountains again.

With a nod to the mountains, I drew my cloak tighter around my shoulders. The journey ahead looms large, echoing the sorrow of our loss. There was no time to mourn; our path called us forward, our duty as unyielding as the mountains themselves. We marched on, leaving behind Yggdrasil, bearing the weight of our victory, and the memory of Thorkel.

We trudged along the worn trail leading us back southward. The hush of the wild around us was eerie, a silent witness to our solemn march. Every crackling leaf under our feet, every whisper of the wind through the trees, felt like the world mirroring our own disquiet.

Out of the silence, Astrid's voice emerged, brimming with worry. "Eirikstorp..." she began, her tone riddled with apprehension, "The Vendelings are still embroiled in the conflict with the Skjoldungs, the Geatish tribes to the east. I fear what we might find when we return."

Her words hanged heavy in the cool air, painting a picture of unrest and war. It was a sharp contrast to the serene forest around us, a jarring reminder of the world's turmoil beyond our immediate vision. Her emerald eyes flashed with anxiety, reflecting the fire of her spirit and the weight of her responsibility.

Looking at her, I found my thoughts echoing her fears. "Hopefully, we'll find the latest news when we reach the nearest village," I said, my voice strained with anticipation. The uncertainty gnawed at me, a cruel reminder of our constant battle against time and fate.

Erik, our quiet pillar, turned to us then. "My village isn't far from here. Stay at my home before we continue to Eirikstorp." His words served as a beacon in the thick fog of our concerns, a promise of temporary respite.

Astrid and I exchanged glances. We both nodded at Erik, accepting his generous offer. As we altered our course towards Erik's village, the prospect of a brief sanctuary in these trying times felt like a beacon of hope. For now, it was a beacon we desperately cling to as we pressed onwards, carrying our private fears and shared grief with us down the winding road.

After days of journeying, the silhouette of Valgarda emerged on the horizon. The village, set in a verdant valley and framed by towering pines, was a welcome sight. The ache of travel ebbed as we drew closer, our spirits lifted by the prospect of rest and a moment's respite.

As we approached the entrance, a murmur swept through the villagers. Eyes widened and hushed whispers grew louder as Erik, their solitary hunter, strode into the village not alone, but accompanied by two strangers. The air was thick with curiosity and a spark of apprehension; it was clear Erik's usual solitude had been replaced with unexpected company.

One of the villagers, a stout man with a weathered face, stepped forward. "Erik," he greeted, casting a wary eye over Astrid and me. "The darkness that surrounded our lands has dissipated." The man's voice was rough as an oak bark, each word resonating with a hint of wonder and relief. "Do you know what happened?"

Erik's response was a hearty laugh, his blue eyes twinkling with mischief. "I'll sing you a tale," he declared, a playful smirk tugging at the corners of his lips. "A tale of Brunhilde and her brave companions, who fought the darkness and won."

His words hung in the air, a promise of an exciting story. Yet, he carefully kept our identities hidden, choosing to shroud us in the anonymity of his narrative. The villagers, none the wiser, clung to his words, their faces lighting up at the prospect of a story of such magnitude.

That night, as laughter and tales of victory echoed from the hall where Erik and Astrid celebrated, I sought the solitude of my room. The door creaked shut behind me, cutting off the din of the celebration and leaving me in welcomed silence. My head was heavy with fatigue, my body ached from the journey, and my heart was still weighed down by the burden of Thorkel's absence. The bed was a simple affair, but it offered comfort and the promise of rest.

As I drifted into the realm of dreams, the darkness of sleep was disrupted by an ethereal glow. The Norns, those divine beings known to weave the threads of fate, emerged within my dream. Their appearances were as they had always been – the eldest with her silver hair cascading down like a waterfall, her eyes holding centuries of wisdom. The middle one, beautiful and stern, her fingers ceaselessly moving, weaving the threads of destiny. And the youngest, her gaze filled with the innocence and cruelty of impending fate.

They floated around me, their ethereal bodies glowing, casting shifting shadows around the dream realm. A chill ran down my spine, a sense of foreboding washing over me. Something was amiss. The Norns, they did not visit without reason.

In unison, they spoke, their voices a haunting melody that echoed in the vast expanse of my dream. "The Veil of Vanir has awakened." The words hung heavy in the air, their implications seeping into the corners of my consciousness.

They continued, "Your battle with Fafnir, the aftershocks of your victory, they have disturbed the ancient one. With Yggdrasil weakened, the Veil threatens to envelop the nine realms, leading all into oblivion."

Their words hit me like a wave crashing on the shore. I jolted awake, my heart pounding against my chest like a drum of war. Cold sweat trickled down my face, soaking the sheets, my breaths coming in ragged gasps. For a moment, I laid there, caught between the world of dreams and the harsh reality.

I shook my head, the afterimage of the Norns still burning behind my eyelids. It was just a dream, I tried to convince myself. The lingering dread, however, gnawed at the edge of my thoughts, refusing to be dismissed. With a sigh, I pushed away the unsettling feelings and forced my eyes shut, willing myself back into the sweet oblivion of sleep.

I couldn't. Deep down, I knew another prophecy had just come to me. And just like before, they needed me.

Read the next story in:
Brunhilde: Veil of Vanir

Printed in Great Britain
by Amazon